RIDE 'EM, TRAILSMAN!

The next moment, Fargo managed to get his right leg up and hook it in front of Sabin's neck. Fargo kicked hard, sending Sabin sprawling in the dust. Fargo rolled, came up on his hands and knees, and leaped onto Sabin's back. His right arm went around Sabin's neck. His left hand clamped on his right wrist. His forearm was like a bar of iron as he locked it across Sabin's throat.

Caught out of breath like he was, Sabin was desperate for air. He heaved his body upward, trying to throw Fargo off, but Fargo had his legs wrapped around Sabin's waist by now and wasn't going anywhere. Sabin managed to lurch to his feet. The mule skinner stumbled back and forth and flailed at Fargo. None of the blows connected with enough power behind them to do any good. Sabin grew weaker with every second that went by.

Finally, Sabin's knees buckled. He toppled forward like a tree, and landed with a crash like falling timber. . . .

TEXAS TRACKDOWN

by

Jon Sharpe

A SIGNET BOOK

SIGNET
Published by New American Library, a division of
Penguin Group (USA) Inc., 375 Hudson Street,
New York, New York 10014, USA
Penguin Group (Canada), 90 Eglinton Avenue East, Suite 700, Toronto,
Ontario M4P 2Y3, Canada (a division of Pearson Penguin Canada Inc.)
Penguin Books Ltd., 80 Strand, London WC2R 0RL, England
Penguin Ireland, 25 St. Stephen's Green, Dublin 2,
Ireland (a division of Penguin Books Ltd.)
Penguin Group (Australia), 250 Camberwell Road, Camberwell, Victoria 3124,
Australia (a division of Pearson Australia Group Pty. Ltd.)
Penguin Books India Pvt. Ltd., 11 Community Centre, Panchsheel Park,
New Delhi - 110 017, India
Penguin Group (NZ), 67 Apollo Drive, Rosedale, North Shore 0632,
New Zealand (a division of Pearson New Zealand Ltd.)
Penguin Books (South Africa) (Pty.) Ltd., 24 Sturdee Avenue,
Rosebank, Johannesburg 2196, South Africa

Penguin Books Ltd., Registered Offices:
80 Strand, London WC2R 0RL, England

First published by Signet, an imprint of New American Library,
a division of Penguin Group (USA) Inc.

First Printing, December 2009
10 9 8 7 6 5 4 3 2 1

The first chapter of this book previously appeared in *Silver Showdown*, the three hundred thirty-seventh volume in this series.

Printed in the United States of America

The Trailsman

Beginnings . . . they bend the tree and they mark the man. Skye Fargo was born when he was eighteen. Terror was his midwife, vengeance his first cry. Killing spawned Skye Fargo, ruthless, cold-blooded murder. Out of the acrid smoke of gunpowder still hanging in the air, he rose, cried out a promise never forgotten.

The Trailsman they began to call him all across the West: searcher, scout, hunter, the man who could see where others only looked, his skills for hire but not his soul, the man who lived each day to the fullest, yet trailed each tomorrow. Skye Fargo, the Trailsman, the seeker who could take the wildness of a land and the wanting of a woman and make them his own.

Texas, 1860—where danger for the Trailsman lurks in the untamed land beyond the Brazos.

1

The sound of a ruckus somewhere nearby made the big man in buckskins narrow his lake blue eyes. He paused on the steps of the brick courthouse in Weatherford, Texas, and looked for the source of the commotion.

The shouting came from a saloon on the south side of the courthouse square. Men hurried in that direction to see what was going on. Just as one hombre reached the saloon's entrance, the batwings flew open and made him jerk back. A man came backward out of the saloon, stumbling on the rough planks of the boardwalk as he tried to keep his balance.

He failed in that effort and landed in the street. A small cloud of dust rose around him from the impact. He shook his head, evidently trying to clear some of the cobwebs from his brain.

On the courthouse steps, Skye Fargo leaned against the railing and folded his arms across his broad, muscular chest. A faint smile touched his wide mouth as he shook his head. Some folks just shouldn't patronize saloons. They always got into trouble when they drank. Evidently, the fella who'd landed in the street was one of them.

A man slapped the batwings aside and stalked out of the saloon. Two more men followed closely behind him. The first man was big, with massive shoulders and long arms. A black beard jutted from his chin and hung down over his chest. He stepped into the street, reached down and grabbed the fallen man's shirt.

Fargo's eyes narrowed even more as the big man hit his

victim twice, back-and-forth blows with a malletlike fist across the hombre's face. Then the man drew back his foot and kicked that unfortunate son in the belly. He kicked him again, making his body bow up and then roll through the dust. The big man's companions stood on the boardwalk in front of the saloon, laughing and yelling encouragement.

"Go get him, Sabin!"

"Stomp his guts out!"

Shaking his head again, Fargo went down the steps to the hitch rail in front of the courthouse. He reached for the reins of a magnificent black-and-white Ovaro stallion tied there.

"Stop it! Get away from him!"

The sound of a woman's voice shouting in anger and fear made Fargo pause and turn his head to look toward the saloon again. The woman was rushing toward the violence in the street from a general store also on that side of the square. Her sunbonnet had slipped down, revealing blond hair. She was young, no more than twenty or so.

She tried to get between the big man called Sabin and the man he had knocked down. Her fists flailed at him. Sabin snarled and clamped a hamlike hand on her shoulder. He flung her out of his way like a rag doll. With a cry of pain, the young woman sprawled in the street, too.

When Fargo saw that, his jaw clenched under the close-cropped dark beard. Instead of untying the Ovaro's reins, he patted the horse on the shoulder as he strode past and said, "I'll be back."

The distraction provided by the young woman had given the man in the street time to struggle to his feet. He was young, too, maybe twenty-five, with curly brown hair. As Sabin turned toward him again, he lunged forward and swung a fist at the bigger man's head.

Sabin slapped aside the blow before it reached its target and then hooked a punch into the young man's belly. He laughed, grabbed the young man's shoulders, and head-butted him in the face. Blood welled from the man's nose. He collapsed when Sabin let go of him.

"Now comes the real stompin'." Sabin lifted a foot and poised it, ready to drive his boot heel down into the young man's face.

Fargo's voice came from behind him. "I don't think so. Leave him alone."

One of Sabin's friends on the boardwalk called out a warning, "Watch out, Sabin!"

The big man looked around anyway, just in time for Fargo's fist to explode on his jaw. Fargo was several inches shorter and thirty or forty pounds lighter than Sabin, but he packed a lot of strength into his powerful frame. The punch landed cleanly and sent Sabin flying off his feet. He crashed down in the dirt street, just like the man he had been beating.

Fargo flexed his fingers to make sure he hadn't busted anything in his hand. Everything seemed to still be working properly.

Sabin's friends stared as if they were unable to believe that anybody had knocked the big man down. Their eyes bugged out even more when Sabin tried to get up and failed. He slumped back down with a groan.

Even so, Fargo didn't turn his back on the man. He kept his eyes on Sabin as he angled toward the young man and woman. Another woman had appeared, probably coming from the general store as well, and with an anxious look on her face now knelt beside the blonde. This one was younger, eighteen or so, and had light brown hair in braids.

"Jessie, are you all right?" the brunette asked. She looked over at the young man. "Oh, Whit, what have you done now?"

With help, the blonde sat up. She brushed some of the dust off the front of her dress, which pulled the calico fabric tighter and emphasized the curve of her breasts.

"I'm fine. Stop fussing over me, Emily. Whit's the one who's hurt."

She got to her feet, and the two young women went over to the young man called Whit. Fargo had gotten a good enough look at all three of them to recognize the family resemblance. The young women had to be sisters, and Whit was their brother.

Quite a few people had gathered to watch the fracas. Now that it was over, they started to drift away. That didn't surprise Fargo. None of them had stepped forward to help Whit. All they had been interested in was watching.

Fargo gave a polite tug on the broad brim of his brown hat as he stepped up to the two young women. "Ladies. Let me give you a hand with this fella."

"Thank you." The blonde managed to flash a quick smile at him, but she still looked upset and worried. "I hope he's not hurt too bad."

Fargo reached down, got his hands under Whit's arms, and lifted him to his feet. The lower half of the young man's face was smeared with blood, but at least his nose didn't appear to be broken. He was lucky in that respect.

Whit swayed and would have fallen, but Fargo still had hold of him and kept him upright.

"He probably needs to sit down somewhere."

The brunette pointed and said, "That's our wagon over there."

Fargo steered Whit toward the vehicle. Whit was pretty unsteady, but with Fargo's help, he made it to the wagon. The tailgate was already down, so Fargo sat him on it and kept a hand on his shoulder to steady him.

"Emily, you go see if you can get a wet cloth so we can clean him up." The blonde gave the order like she was used to being in charge. She looked at Fargo and went on. "I'll stay here with Mr. . . . ?"

"Fargo. Skye Fargo."

"I'm Jessie Franklin. That's my sister, Emily, and this is our brother, Whit."

Fargo smiled. "I'd say that I'm pleased to meet you, Miss Franklin, but under the circumstances . . ."

"Well, *I'm* pleased," Jessie said. "If you hadn't come along, that monster might have killed poor Whit."

Fargo hadn't smelled any liquor on Whit's breath as he was helping the young man over to the wagon. He asked, "Do you have any idea what started the fight?"

"Unfortunately, I do." Jessie Franklin took a deep breath. "I'm afraid I did."

Sabin's companions stepped down from the boardwalk and hurried over to their fallen friend. One of them, a little, fox-faced man, reached down and shook his shoulder.

"Sabin! Sabin, you better get up and whale the tar outta that bastard. Sabin!"

The big man just groaned again. The one who had just tried to rouse him looked over at the third man and said, "We got to do somethin' about this!"

The third man shook his head, with a dour expression on his saturnine face. "Did you see the way that fella walloped Sabin? I don't want any part of that. Let's just pick him up, get him back in the saloon, and pour a drink down his throat. That's what he needs."

The second man took his battered old hat off and scratched his head, which was covered with lank, fair hair. "Well, all right, but it don't set well with me, lettin' that varmint get away with hittin' our compadre like that."

"Come on, Martin. Quit your bellyachin' and give me a hand with him."

Together, they struggled to lift the semiconscious Sabin to his feet, and then the three of them staggered off toward the saloon. Once they were inside, Martin and the third man helped Sabin sit down at an empty table. Martin handed a coin to his companion.

"Go get us a bottle, Jackson."

"Sure."

Martin took one of the other chairs at the table while Jackson went off to the bar. Sabin pressed his palms against the table for support as he ponderously shook his head.

"What the hell happened out there?" he said.

Martin leaned forward eagerly. "Some big fella in buckskins coldcocked you, that's what happened. Don't you remember?"

"I don't remember nothin' except goin' out in the street to teach that damn Franklin kid a lesson."

Martin licked his lips. "Well, this other hombre, he came up and hit you from behind. With a two-by-four."

Sabin took hold of his bearded jaw and gingerly worked it back and forth. "If he hit me from behind, how come it's my jaw that hurts?" His voice was thick with pain.

"That's because he, uh, he came up on you from behind, but then you turned around just as he swung that board at your head."

"Oh." Sabin frowned. "What happened to the kid?"

"He went off with the fella that walloped you. And those pretty little sisters of his."

Jackson came back from the bar with a bottle of whiskey and three glasses. "Martin, you ain't agitatin' again, are you?" he asked as he thumped the bottle and glasses down on the table. "I swear, you like to stir things up more'n anybody I ever saw."

"I was just tellin' Sabin here about how that other fella came up and hit him from behind with a two-by-four." Martin looked meaningfully at Jackson as he spoke.

"What? Oh. Yeah." There was a resigned tone to Jackson's voice now. "A two-by-four."

Sabin spoke with a rumble like thunder. "Well, hell. I can't let him get away with that."

"You sure can't." Martin grinned. "Want me to go see if I can find him for you so you can settle the score?"

Sabin reached for the bottle. "Maybe in a little while. I got to get some of this Who-hit-John in me first. I got a devil of a headache." He splashed some of the fiery liquor in a glass, then threw back the drink. He ran his tongue around his whiskery mouth to collect any stray drops. "But he ain't gonna get away with it. That's for damned sure."

Fargo smiled at Jessie Franklin. "You don't look like the sort who goes around starting ruckuses."

Jessie sighed and shook her head. "That shows you how little you know about me, Mr. Fargo."

"I don't know much of anything about you, except your name."

Whit groaned and hunched over as he sat on the tailgate. "I feel like I been kicked by a mule, Jessie."

"Next thing to it," she said. "Aaron Sabin kicked you, and then he punched you in the belly."

Whit frowned. "That big mule skinner?" His expression cleared. "Oh, yeah. For a minute I hurt so bad, I couldn't remember what happened. I went over to the saloon to tell him to leave you alone." Whit grimaced in pain again. "He didn't take kindly to it."

Emily came out of the store with a bucket of water in one hand and a piece of cloth in the other. "Mr. Higginbotham said we could use this to clean up Whit." She set the bucket on the tailgate next to her brother.

Jessie took the cloth, got it wet, and began wiping away the blood from Whit's face. He made pained noises and tried to turn his head away. Jessie slapped him on the leg.

"Stop that," she ordered. "Let me get this cleaned up."

"All right, all right. Just take it easy, will you? My nose hurts, too."

"What did you expect, brawling with somebody like Sabin? He's twice your size, and you know how mean he is."

"You heard what he said about you. Him and those two friends of his standin' in front of the saloon and making nasty comments to girls. Don't they have anything better to do?"

A pink glow of embarrassment spread over Jessie's lightly freckled face. "Evidently not. Still, you didn't have to go charging over there to defend my honor like some . . . some knight in shining armor."

Her eyes flicked toward Fargo as she said that.

"You say this fella Sabin is a mule skinner?" Fargo asked.

"Yes. He and his friends work for the freight line that runs between here and Fort Worth. They're no-good troublemakers, all three of them." A shudder ran through Jessie. "Especially that little one, Martin. When he looks at me, it's like . . . a snake watching me."

Fargo knew what she meant. He had run into hombres like that. You looked in their eyes and there was nothing there, just black emptiness.

Whit said to Fargo, "Thanks for helpin' me over here to the wagon, mister."

"He didn't help you over here," Jessie said. "Emily and I did that. He knocked out Sabin."

Whit stared. "He did what?"

"Stepped up and told Sabin to leave you alone. And then when Sabin turned around, Mr. Fargo hit him harder than I've ever seen a man hit anybody."

Fargo shrugged. "A lucky punch." It wasn't really all that lucky, of course. He had punched plenty of troublemaking hombres in the past.

Whit's forehead creased in a worried frown. He pushed Jessie's hand with the wet rag away from his face and looked around.

"Where's Sabin now?"

"Martin and Jackson got him on his feet and helped him into the saloon. Now let me finish cleaning that blood off, Whit."

Instead of doing as Jessie told him, Whit pushed off the tailgate and stood up behind the wagon. "Mr. . . . Fargo, is it? Mr. Fargo, you better watch out. You may have gotten in a lucky punch, but that won't stop Aaron Sabin for long. He'll come after you. He'll feel like he's got a score to settle with you for interfering with him."

"That's up to him, I reckon."

"No, you don't understand. You need to get out of town."

Fargo just looked at him. "You mean run?"

"No, just . . . Well, yeah. Sabin's loco, especially with that little weasel Martin eggin' him on." Whit's expression suddenly brightened. "I know. Come back out to the ranch with us."

Jessie shook her head before Fargo could respond. "That's not a good idea, Whit. If Sabin can't find Mr. Fargo in town, Lost Valley is the first place he'll look." She turned to Fargo. "That's where our ranch is. Our mother's ranch, I should say. And it's not that we wouldn't want you to visit, but—"

Fargo nodded. "You don't want to bring even more trouble down on your heads."

"That's right." Jessie sounded relieved. "You understand."

"Sure." Fargo glanced into the wagon bed and saw several crates and burlap bags. "You folks came into town for supplies, right? If you're finished with your shopping, maybe you'd better head on back home."

"Yes, I think that would be best."

Whit didn't see it that way, though. "We can't just leave Mr. Fargo here to face Sabin and his bunch alone."

Jessie cast a quick glance up and down Fargo's buckskin-clad body. "I think Mr. Fargo can probably take care of himself."

Emily rolled her eyes and shook her head. She took the wet cloth away from Jessie, dipped it in the water again, and proceeded to finish swabbing away the dried blood on her brother's face.

"Hold still, Whit," she told him. "I'll be done here in a minute, and then we can go."

Whit let out a little groan. "Too late. Here comes Sabin."

Fargo turned and saw that Whit was right. The burly mule skinner had just emerged from the saloon. The batwings were still swinging back and forth behind him. He stalked toward the wagon, with his two friends following close behind him. The smaller man, Martin, was bouncing up and down on the balls of his feet in obvious excitement.

Sabin pointed a finger at Fargo and bellowed, "Hold it right there!"

Fargo hooked his thumbs in his belt and smiled thinly. "I'm not planning on going anywhere."

"Good, 'cause I got a bone to pick with you. What do you mean, comin' up behind a fella like that and cloutin' him with a two-by-four?"

A startled exclamation came from Jessie. "A two-by-four! Why, Mr. Fargo didn't hit you with anything except his fist!"

Sabin scowled at her. "That ain't true. It can't be. No man's ever laid me out with one punch before." His murderous glare moved over to Fargo. "How about it?"

"There's a first time for everything."

Sabin looked like he was going to argue, but then he paused

and reached up to massage his jaw. "You know, it *feels* like somebody punched me." He lowered his hand and clenched both of them into fists at his side. "But that don't change anything. You still Injuned up on me."

Fargo shook his head. "I walked up and told you to stop beating on this young fella. And I might have stayed out of it, even then, if you hadn't laid hands on his sister."

For a second, Sabin looked like he didn't know what Fargo was talking about. Then his lip curled in a sneer as he remembered.

"She should'a stayed outta my way. I don't let no female tell me what to do."

"What you should be saying is that you apologize for throwing her down."

A braying laugh came from Martin. "What the hell would he want to do that for? Sabin ain't the first hombre to throw that little hussy down, let me tell you."

Whit took a step toward him. "Why, you—"

"Stop him, Sabin!" Martin dodged behind the bigger man. "Don't let him get me!"

Sabin's right fist swung and would have connected with Whit's face if Fargo hadn't grabbed the back of the young man's collar and jerked him out of the way. He shoved Whit into the arms of Jessie and Emily.

"The three of you get in the store."

Sabin grinned through his bushy beard at Fargo and smacked his right fist into the palm of his left hand. "This is more like it. Just you and me, mister. And this time we'll settle things."

With a roar, he lunged at Fargo, swinging wide, looping punches. Sabin was strong as an ox, but he was slow. Fargo ducked under those blows and hammered a left into Sabin's midsection. Unfortunately, that didn't really slow the man down much. Momentum carried him forward. He crashed into Fargo and drove him backward against the sideboards of the wagon.

Fargo's lips drew back from his teeth. He brought his fists in and slammed them against Sabin's ears. Sabin howled in pain. He hunched his head down between his shoulders and tried to butt Fargo in the face, but Fargo had seen him do the same thing to Whit Franklin and was ready for the move. He twisted aside, grabbed Sabin's thatch of black hair, and rammed the mule skinner's face against the sideboards.

Sabin let out another roar, sounding like a cross between a grizzly bear and a maddened bull. He pulled back, but Fargo was ready for that, too. Fargo's fist came whistling up in an uppercut that landed on Sabin's chin and clicked his teeth together hard. Sabin stumbled back a couple of steps.

Martin was starting to look nervous. "Don't let him do that to you, Sabin! You're bigger'n him! Rip his head off!"

Sabin was big and strong, all right, but it was clear that his size and strength had always been enough for him to win his fights. He had no real skill with his fists. Fargo stepped in and peppered a wicked combination to Sabin's face, opening up a cut on the man's cheek. Sabin yelled and shook his head, spraying crimson droplets around it. He swung another sledgehammer punch that Fargo easily avoided.

"Martin! Jackson! Grab this son of a bitch and make him hold still!"

Neither of the two men leaped to answer Sabin's plea for help. Sabin charged again, not punching now but spreading his arms wide instead. Fargo couldn't avoid their long reach. Sabin caught him, and the two of them went rolling in the dirt of the courthouse square.

Quite a crowd had gathered again as soon as the fight broke out. Some men cheered for Sabin, while others rooted against him. Fargo didn't really know anyone here, so nobody was for or against him.

As the bystanders formed a rough circle around them, the two men came to a stop. Sabin was on top, and he grinned hugely as he used his weight to pin Fargo to the ground and tried to wrap his sausagelike fingers around Fargo's neck. Fargo got his left hand under Sabin's chin and forced his head back, holding him off for the moment.

Fargo shot a punch into Sabin's solar plexus. The blow didn't travel very far, maybe six inches, but Fargo's fist sunk almost to the wrist. Sabin reared back and started choking and gasping. Fargo's punch had driven all the air out of his lungs.

The next moment, Fargo managed to get his right leg up and hook it in front of Sabin's neck. Fargo kicked hard with that leg. The move threw Sabin off and sent him sprawling in the dust. Fargo rolled over, came up on his hands and knees, and leaped onto Sabin's back. His right arm went around Sabin's neck. His left hand clamped on his right wrist. His forearm was like a bar of iron as he locked it across Sabin's throat.

Caught out of breath like he was, within heartbeats Sabin was desperate for air. He heaved his body upward, trying to throw Fargo off, but Fargo had his legs wrapped around Sabin's waist by now and wasn't going anywhere. Sabin managed to lurch to his feet. He clawed at Fargo's grip but couldn't loosen it. The mule skinner stumbled back and forth and flailed at Fargo. None of the blows connected with enough power behind them to do any good. Sabin grew weaker with every second that went by.

Finally, Sabin's knees buckled. He toppled forward like a tree falling, and landed with a crash like falling timber, too. Fargo let go of him and stood up. His chest rose and fell heavily from the exertion of the past few minutes.

Then Whit Franklin was beside him, slapping him on the back. "Man alive! I never saw such a fight! Lucky punch, hell! You beat Sabin fair and square! Nobody ever beat him before!"

Fargo looked around. Sabin appeared to be out cold again, for the second time in less than an hour, but Martin and Jackson were still conscious and might represent a threat.

Fargo spotted the two of them standing in the forefront of the crowd. Martin stared in disbelief at Sabin's senseless form. Jackson just looked disgusted by the whole affair.

Fargo's hat had fallen off during the fight. He picked it up and slapped it against his thigh to get some of the dust off of it as he approached Martin and Jackson.

"Am I going to have trouble with you fellas, too?"

Jackson shook his head. "Not me, mister. I didn't think anybody could whip Sabin in a fair fight, but you did it."

Fargo turned to Martin. "You. You're the one who told him I clobbered him with a two-by-four, aren't you?"

Martin swallowed hard. "I . . . I don't know what you're talkin' about."

"When he wakes up, tell him the truth. My good name means enough to me that I don't want even the likes of him going around thinking that I'd do a thing like that."

"Your name? What the hell *is* your name?"

"Skye Fargo."

Jackson's eyes widened in recognition. "The Trailsman?"

Fargo nodded. "That's right."

Jackson began to laugh. "I've heard of you, mister. Sabin's lucky to be alive. They say you're one of the most dangerous hombres on the frontier."

"They say a lot of things . . . but not that I sneak up on a man and hit him with a piece of timber. Remember that."

Fargo fastened a cold, slit-eyed stare on Martin for a second, then turned away.

He came face-to-face with the yawning twin barrels of a scattergun.

2

The man holding the greener had a red, weathered face and a black mustache that drooped over his mouth. He was only medium-sized, but he didn't seem to be having any trouble holding the shotgun rock steady. A badge pinned to the lapel of his sober black suit gleamed in the sunlight.

"All right, what the hell's—" The lawman's agitated question came to an abrupt end when he recognized the man he was looking at over the barrels of the shotgun. "Fargo?"

"That's right, Sheriff."

Fargo had been visiting with Sheriff Tate Laughlin in the Parker County courthouse less than an hour earlier. He had never met the man before today, but they had a mutual friend, an army major named Stilwell. The major had asked Fargo to stop by and say howdy to Laughlin for him, the next time he was down this way, and Fargo had done so.

Laughlin lowered the shotgun and looked past Fargo at Aaron Sabin's senseless form stretched out in the street. "That can't be who I think it is." He glanced at Martin and Jackson and then spat disgustedly. "Or I reckon maybe it is, since there are the other two troublemakers who are always with him."

Jackson shook his head. "Not me, Sheriff. I didn't have anything to do with this."

Martin glared at him. "I thought you was our friend."

"I am, but I don't aim to get locked up for something I didn't do."

Sheriff Laughlin stepped forward. "I didn't say I was lockin' anybody up. I want to know what's goin' on, though. Somebody told me there was a ruckus out here a while ago. Were you mixed up in that, too, Fargo?"

"You didn't hear all the yelling?"

"I was in a county commissioners' meeting." Laughlin shook his head. "That was all the yellin' I could hear."

Jessie Franklin said, "The fight wasn't Mr. Fargo's fault, Sheriff."

Whit moved around her to face the lawman. "That's right," he said. "It was mine. I started it when I went after Sabin for makin' ugly comments about my sister."

Laughlin tucked the shotgun under his arm. "Then it sounds to me like Sabin started it." He chuckled. "And he got the worst of it, looks like. Did you do that, Fargo?"

Fargo shrugged.

"Sabin's always gettin' in fights, but none of 'em ever ended up like this before." Laughlin looked around at the crowd and snapped an order. "Some of you men pick him up and carry him around to the jail."

That brought a protest from Martin. "You can't arrest Sabin! He was just defendin' himself. That fella Fargo hit him first."

Laughlin looked at Fargo again. "Is that true?"

Fargo nodded. "Yeah, I hit him before he hit me . . . but *after* he started giving Whit Franklin a thrashing and threw Miss Jessie down in the dirt."

The sheriff glared at Martin. "That don't sound like no case of self-defense to me. You want to be locked up for disturbin' the peace, too?"

Martin licked his lips and shook his head. "No, sir, I sure don't. I, uh, I reckon I just didn't see the whole thing like I thought I did."

"Hmmph. I reckon not." Laughlin jerked a thumb toward Sabin. "Get him to the jail. My deputy'll know what to do with him."

Reluctantly, several men stepped forward to follow the sheriff's orders. They picked up Sabin and lugged him around the courthouse, out of sight.

Laughlin turned back to the Trailsman and the three Franklin siblings. "Any of you folks want to press charges?"

Fargo shook his head. So did Whit.

"Just let it go, Sheriff," Whit said. "The girls and I just want to get back out to the ranch in peace."

Laughlin nodded. "All right, then. That's fine. I'll keep him locked up overnight, and in the morning the judge can fine him five dollars for disturbin' the peace. Maybe after that he'll go back to Fort Worth where he belongs."

Weatherford was some thirty miles west of Fort Worth, which was older by a few years, larger, and had a reputation as a rough place. Weatherford, though, was right on the very edge of civilized Texas. The next settlement to the west was Fort Griffin, and in between was the Brazos River and the Palo Pinto country, an area of rough, wooded, rocky hills and dark, desolate valleys.

At certain times of year, those hills were crawling with Comanches, too. Fargo had heard stories about the hostiles raiding within a mile or two of Weatherford. Some people worried that one of these days, a veritable army of Comanch' might come down out of the Panhandle and attack Weatherford itself, maybe even Fort Worth and Dallas. About a dozen years earlier, the Indians had carried out a raid like that, sweeping all the way to the Gulf Coast and spreading death and destruction everywhere along the way.

Fargo didn't believe that such a large, coordinated raid would happen again anytime soon, if ever. Due to his contacts with the army, he knew that the Indians had been pressed and harried more than most people suspected. That fact, along with the natural rivalries between the various tribes and even different bands of the same tribe, made it difficult for their leaders to put together a large force.

But it wasn't out of the question, and anyway, smaller war parties could do plenty of damage with their hit-and-run strikes. Living anywhere west of the Trinity River was chancy. Living west of the Brazos was a flat-out dangerous proposition.

Jessie had said that the Franklin ranch was located in some place called Lost Valley. Fargo didn't know where that was, but it sounded pretty remote. Since Sabin was going to be locked up, at least for tonight, maybe it would be a good idea if he visited the ranch, after all.

"You don't need me for anything, Sheriff?" he asked.

Laughlin shook his head. "Nope, nothing I can think of."

Fargo turned to Whit and clapped a hand on the young man's shoulder. "I reckon I'll take you up on that invitation to pay a visit to your ranch. If it still stands, that is."

Whit grinned. "Of course it does." Then he glanced at Jessie. "Doesn't it?"

Even though he was the oldest of the siblings, it was pretty obvious which one of them was really in charge.

Jessie hesitated, then nodded and smiled at Fargo. "I think that would be all right."

"I'll get my horse."

By the time he untied the Ovaro from the hitch rail and led the stallion back over to the wagon, Jessie and Whit had climbed onto the seat. Whit held the reins that were hitched to a team of four mules. Emily had climbed into the uncovered back and sat on one of the crates of supplies.

Fargo swung up into the saddle as Whit turned the wagon around. The young man slapped the reins against the backs of the team until the mules began to plod forward. Wherever they were going, they wouldn't be in any hurry to get there.

But that was fine with Fargo. He didn't have any place he had to be. He glanced at Jessie Franklin, who still wore her bonnet back so that her blond hair shone like gold in the sun, and smiled as he hitched the Ovaro into motion.

The terrain just west of Weatherford was fairly level and easy traveling for several miles. There were occasional steep hills, but most of them rolled gently. Stands of post oak, live oak, and cedar dotted the hills, and tall cottonwoods lined the banks of the frequent creeks. It was pretty country, not much good for farming but fair ranch land.

The farther west Fargo and his companions went, though, the more rugged the landscape became. The trail they followed wound through the hills and from time to time climbed through passes that gave spectacular views of the Texas countryside. Just looking at those views, most people might not suspect how much danger lurked out there.

But it was there, all right, painted and feathered, waiting to strike unwary pilgrims. For that reason, Fargo kept both eyes wide open. He rode with the Ovaro's reins in his left hand, and his right hand was never far from the walnut grips of the Colt holstered on his hip. The Henry repeating rifle in the saddle boot was fully loaded, too, if he needed it.

He edged the stallion closer to the wagon. "Where's this Lost Valley you mentioned?"

Jessie turned her head to smile at him. "Just on the other side of the Brazos, close to where it makes that big bend."

"That's Comanche country."

"I know. But they've never bothered us. We've found tracks where war parties have passed through, but for some reason they've never raided our ranch."

They had been lucky so far. That luck couldn't last.

"Maybe you should give some thought to moving closer to town," Fargo suggested.

Jessie shrugged. "Ma doesn't want to. She's lived there for a long time, she says, and she's not going to let the Indians make her run away."

"Your mother sounds like a stubborn woman."

Whit laughed. "Now you know where Jessie gets it."

She glared at him. "It's not being stubborn if you're right all the time. It's just being practical."

"Yeah, I reckon you could look at it like that." Whit was still grinning.

From the back of the wagon, Emily spoke up. "Don't you two start in again. I swear, the way you squabble sometimes makes me think *I'm* the oldest, instead of the youngest."

The wagon couldn't move very fast, so it took most of the day to reach the Brazos River. Fargo learned that the three of them had traveled to Weatherford the day before. Lost Valley was too far away to make the trip to town and back in the same day.

Late that afternoon, they crested a rise and started down a long, gentle slope toward a line of greenery that marked the river's course. Fargo gestured toward it as they approached.

"I recall that there's a ford up here," he said. "You have to be careful of quicksand, though."

Whit nodded. "That's right. We've been across it plenty of times, though, so I know where to drive."

"Is old Paul Washburn still hauling freight through here, out to Fort Griffin?" Fargo had helped map out that freight line and, as usual, had run into plenty of trouble along the way.

"No, he retired, and that fella Sparks who helped him passed away. There's no freight line through these parts now. Nothing but army supply wagons go past Weatherford."

And it was likely to remain that way, too, until the threat from the Comanches was dealt with.

The trail led down a section of riverbank that wasn't too steep. The river was shallow here most of the time, although spring thunderstorms could cause it to flood. Right now, much of the sandy bed was visible because it had been a dry summer. Whit sent the mules out onto a section where the sand was packed hard enough to support the wagon.

Fargo followed on the Ovaro. His eyes scanned the wooded hills that rose on both sides of the river, searching for any signs of trouble or danger.

The crossing was uneventful and took only a few minutes. Whit sent the wagon up the western bank. The trail angled off to the northwest.

Fargo frowned and hipped around in the saddle. Once again, he studied the surrounding countryside for a long moment, then shook his head and rode on.

Jessie had turned her head to watch him. "Something wrong?" she asked.

Fargo came up alongside the wagon. "Just a hunch. The hair on the back of my neck said that somebody was watching us. But I don't see anything."

"Then we don't need to worry about it?"

"Sometimes when you *don't* see anything, that's the time to really worry."

As if to emphasize his point, Fargo drew the Henry from its sheath and carried it across the saddle in front of him.

Nothing happened, though, as the wagon continued to roll northwestward. They headed toward a long ridge, but as they came closer, Fargo saw that the ridge wasn't continuous. It just appeared to be from a distance. Actually, it was two ridges that overlapped, with a narrow gap between them. Whit drove through that gap, and when they emerged, Fargo saw a valley between the ridges and a range of hills to the north.

"Lost Valley." It was a guess, but he was confident he was right.

Jessie confirmed that. "It got the name because you can't see the entrance until you're right up on it, and a lot of people pass by without ever knowing it's here."

The valley wasn't large, about a mile wide and maybe three miles long. But that was enough range for a small ranch.

"How many hands do you have working for you?"

Whit grinned. "Hands? There's just the four of us, Mr. Fargo. We raise cattle and a few horses." He inclined his head toward Jessie and Emily. "I hate to say it in front of 'em, but these sisters of mine ride almost as well as I do."

Jessie snorted. "We ride *better* than you."

Emily had to get in on the conversation as well. "We're better shots than you, too."

"Don't listen to 'em, Mr. Fargo. They don't know what they're talkin' about."

Fargo chuckled at the good-natured hoorawing the young

women gave their brother. Whit was probably used to it if he was the only male on a ranch with three females.

A thread of smoke rose into the deep blue sky of late afternoon. Whit steered toward it. A short time later, a cabin came into view, nestled next to some trees only a few yards from a little creek. In a style common to the Texas frontier, it was actually two cabins, linked by a covered area between them known as a dogtrot. As the travelers came closer, Fargo saw that the structure was built of rough-hewn beams instead of logs, but the beams were so thick and heavy, they almost amounted to the same thing.

Each cabin had a chimney at the outside end. The smoke rose from one of them. A couple of big, yellow dogs ran out to meet the wagon, barking furiously as they bounded along. A woman stepped out into the shade of the dogtrot with what appeared to be a rifle cradled in her arms.

"Your mother stayed here alone while the three of you went to Weatherford?" Fargo asked.

Whit laughed in response to the question. "Ma's the best shot of all of us, I reckon."

Jessie and Emily didn't argue with that.

As Fargo rode alongside the wagon, up to the cabin, he saw that Mrs. Franklin was a still-handsome middle-aged woman. Her dark hair had plenty of gray and silver threads in it, and time and the elements had weathered her face, but it was easy to see that once she had been a very beautiful woman. Jessie and Emily must have gotten their good looks from her, although both girls were fairer than their mother was.

Smiling, she stepped out into the late-afternoon sunshine to greet her children. She gave Fargo a slightly suspicious look, though, as she asked, "Who's this?"

"His name is Skye Fargo." Jessie sounded like she enjoyed saying the name. "There was a little trouble in Weatherford this morning, and Mr. Fargo gave us a hand."

"Trouble?" A frown creased Mrs. Franklin's forehead. "What sort of trouble?"

Whit waved a hand. "Nothing to worry about, Ma." The movement made him wince, though. Sabin's kicks had to have bruised his ribs.

"That's not what it looks like to me."

"Whit got in a fight with Aaron Sabin," Emily said.

The young man turned to glare at her. "You're mighty quick to go tellin' stories out of school."

"None of us have been to school in a long time, Whit Franklin." Emily's chin lifted defiantly. "And you're mighty quick to go wading into trouble. You always have been, as far back as I can remember. Just pure-dee reckless. You and Jessie both."

Jessie looked surprised. "Leave me out of this. I'm not the one who tried to fight Sabin—"

"Actually, you did," Emily reminded her. "And you got pushed down for it, too."

"Hold on, hold on." Mrs. Franklin's voice was firm enough to make both her daughters fall silent immediately. "Let's get the wagon unloaded, and then you can tell me all about it. And Mr. Fargo, I'm pleased to meet you. Light and set a spell. I'm obliged to you for helping these young'uns of mine."

Fargo tugged politely on the brim of his hat. "The pleasure's mine, ma'am. And I was glad I could lend a hand during that ruckus in town."

"I've got a pot of coffee on the stove. Would you care for a cup?"

"Yes, ma'am, I certainly would."

"And you'll join us for supper?"

Fargo swung down from the saddle. "It would be my pleasure. I need to care for my horse first, though."

Mrs. Franklin nodded. "I like a man who knows how to take care of a good horse, and this one appears to be a fine animal. Put him in the barn, and come on inside when you're ready."

Fargo had already noticed the good-sized barn built out of the same heavy beams as the house. Someone had put a lot of hard work into this place. The young people hadn't mentioned a father, and Mrs. Franklin was clearly alone here, but there had been a man around at one time. Whit and Jessie had said that the Indians left the ranch alone, so it must have been a fever or some other illness, or maybe some sort of accident, that had claimed Franklin's life.

Half a dozen horses occupied the corral next to the barn. Fargo was a good judge of horseflesh, and he could see that these animals were excellent specimens. If they were indicative of the quality of horses raised by the Franklins, then the ranch was probably doing pretty well. The buildings appeared to be in good repair, too. The family had made a nice home for itself here in Lost Valley.

Fargo led the stallion into the barn. There were several empty stalls, so he put the Ovaro in one, unsaddled him, rubbed him down, and made sure there was grain in the trough and water in the bucket. While he was doing that, Whit brought the mules into the barn and tended to them.

The two men walked back to the house together. Fargo left his saddle in the barn, but he carried his saddlebags and his Henry with him. He wouldn't feel comfortable without the rifle as long as he was on this side of the Brazos.

The sun was almost down. When Fargo and Whit stepped into the left-hand cabin, the delicious smells of coffee brewing and some sort of stew simmering filled the Trailsman's nostrils and brought a grin to his face.

"Nothing like home cooking."

Mrs. Franklin stood stirring the pot of stew that hung over the flames in the fireplace. She nodded at Fargo's comment. "Sit yourself down, Mr. Fargo. Supper's about ready. You'll be staying the night?"

"Yes, ma'am." Fargo took off his hat and hung it on one of the nails driven into the wall for that purpose. "I'm obliged for the hospitality. And call me Skye."

"I'm Grace. You know my children already."

Jessie and Emily were moving around the area set aside as the kitchen, taking china from an old hutch and carrying it to the table, which was covered with a linen cloth. This side of the cabin was comfortably furnished, with the table, a bench on each side, a couple of rocking chairs near the fireplace, and a four-poster bed. The puncheon floor had several woven rugs placed on it.

"The girls have been telling me about what happened in town." Grace gave Whit a stern look. "That was a foolish thing you did, going after Aaron Sabin like that."

"But, Ma, the things he said about Jessie—"

Grace held up a hand to stop him. "Never you mind. You'll just embarrass your sister if you keep going on about it. You should be thankful Mr. Fargo was there to help you."

Whit nodded. "I am. I told him so."

"You'll have to be very careful the next time you go to Weatherford. If you see that man Sabin, you stay away from him. He's the sort to hold a grudge."

"I know." Whit frowned. "I don't much cotton to runnin' away from anybody, though."

"You were always too ready to fight. I'm not telling you to run away. I'm just saying you should try to avoid trouble in the first place."

Whit sighed and nodded. "Yes, ma'am."

With help from Jessie and Emily, Grace began dishing out the stew. It was delicious, filled with chunks of venison, potatoes, and wild onions, and the strong black coffee washed it down perfectly. Fargo mopped every last drop of stew from his bowl with a piece of bread torn from the loaf that sat on a plate in the center of the table.

Night had fallen by the time they finished the meal. Jessie lit several candles with a twig from the fire. Their warm yellow glow filled the room. While Jessie and Emily cleaned up and Whit went outside to feed the dogs and check on the horses, Grace sat in one of the rocking chairs near the fireplace and motioned Fargo into the other one.

"Tell me about yourself, Mr. Fargo."

He smiled. "There's not much to tell. I'm afraid that I'm pretty much a no-account drifter."

"What sort of work do you do?"

"Oh, from time to time I sign on as a wagon train guide, or do some scouting for the army. When I have to, I can come up with a stake by playing a little poker."

Grace's lips pursed. "I don't hold much with card playing. It's not so much that it's sinful itself, but there's usually a lot of sin going on in places where card games are played."

Fargo nodded solemnly. "Yes, ma'am, that's true enough. But I never claimed to be anything except a sinner."

Grace surprised him by chuckling. "You don't have to sound proud of it."

"Well, I don't reckon I am . . . exactly."

Jessie turned her head from the wash pan where she was cleaning the dishes. "In town, one of Sabin's friends said Mr. Fargo is called the Trailsman."

Grace looked at him with more interest. "Really? Is that true?"

Fargo shrugged. "Somebody tagged that name on me a long time ago. It stuck."

"I think I've heard my late husband mention you. You've done quite a bit of work for the army, according to him."

"I like to help out when I can."

"I think you proved that today in Weatherford, when you kept that brute Aaron Sabin from thrashing Whit within an inch of his life."

At that moment, Whit came into the cabin. He wore a worried look on his face as he closed the door.

"The dogs are actin' kind of funny, Ma. I closed the barn doors."

"What do you mean, funny?"

"They kept lookin' off at the hills, like something over there was botherin' 'em."

Fargo sat up straighter in the rocking chair. "Did you see anything over there yourself?"

Whit shook his head. "Nope. Of course, it's pretty dark out there by now."

"Did you hear anything?"

"Just some coyotes."

Jessie came over, drying her hands on a rag. "Coyotes . . . or Comanches?"

"You know the Indians don't bother us." Grace's voice was sharp. "They never have."

Jessie shook her head. "That doesn't mean they never will."

Fargo stood up. "You did good to close the barn doors, Whit, but that won't keep any raiders out if they want in. I reckon I'll stay out there tonight."

Grace got to her feet as well. "That's not necessary, Mr. Fargo. I figured you'd sleep in the loft on the other side of the dogtrot, with Whit."

"I think it'd be better for me to keep an eye on the horses. If any Comanch' do come skulking around, they may not expect to find anybody in the barn." Fargo smiled grimly. "They'll be a mite surprised."

"Why don't I stay out there, too?" Whit said.

Fargo shook his head in response to the suggestion. "You should stay in the cabin. That way we'll have any troublemakers in a cross fire."

Jessie crossed her arms over her chest. "There may not be anything out there. What Whit heard might have been real coyotes."

Fargo smiled and nodded. "Yeah . . . but better not to take the chance." He walked over to the door where he had leaned his Henry against the wall. He picked up the rifle. "I'll head on out there. Good night, folks. Mrs. Franklin . . . Grace . . . I'm obliged for the meal and the hospitality."

"You're welcome, Skye. We're glad to have you here." A little shudder went through her. "Especially tonight."

Fargo nodded and went out. He eased the door closed behind him and was glad to hear the bar being slid into place on the other side of the thick panel. Someone was already closing the shutters on the windows, too.

He walked across the open space between the house and the barn, listening intently as he did so. Night birds called in the trees, and Fargo was experienced enough to recognize the sounds as the real thing.

The coyote yelps in the distance were a different story. He couldn't tell if they were authentic or not. Instinct made his hand tighten on the rifle, though, so there was a good chance they weren't.

Death was afoot out there in the darkness. Fargo felt it in his bones.

The only real question was whether it would come calling in Lost Valley tonight.

3

The Ovaro tossed his head when Fargo came into the barn. Fargo trusted the stallion's instincts as much as he trusted his own. He closed the double front doors and lowered the bar into the hooks, then walked over to the stall where the Ovaro stood with his head high and his nostrils flared.

"I know, big fella. There's trouble out there. We'll meet it as it comes, though, just like we always have."

Fargo made sure the smaller rear door was barred as well. Whit had brought the rest of the horses into the barn and put them in their stalls. Fargo lit the lantern hanging on one of the support posts and looked around the inside of the barn, quickly memorizing every detail about its layout, then blew out the flame.

A thick darkness dropped over the barn's interior, relieved only by a faint grayish glow. That feeble illumination came from the starlight shining through the little door into the hayloft, which was still open.

Fargo went over to the ladder that led up to the loft and climbed it in the dark, feeling his way from rung to rung. By the time he reached the top, his eyes had adjusted and he had no trouble making out the squarish opening above the front doors. He walked over to it, stooping a little because of the low ceiling, and looked out into the night.

The barn faced south, so he couldn't see the hills to the northwest. That was a shame, because he wouldn't be able to see if anyone approached the ranch from that direction, as they most likely would if there was trouble.

But as dark as the night was, with only a sliver of moon, even the keen eyes of the Trailsman wouldn't have been able to see much.

He left the little door open for now and sat down in front of it with his rifle across his knees. He was far enough back so that he was in deep shadow and couldn't be seen easily by anyone looking in from outside.

Like many frontiersmen, he had the ability to rest while remaining alert. If anything happened, he would know about it instantly, even though his eyes had closed to narrow slits.

Time passed. Fargo waited. And the stars wheeled through the sky overhead.

Suddenly, movement caught his eye. A couple of dark shapes emerged from a stand of post oak and darted toward the cabin. At the same time, the dogs leaped up from where they had been dozing in front of the cabin and began to bark.

Up in the hayloft, Fargo lifted the rifle, but before he could fire, a third figure stepped out of the shadows under the gnarled oaks and a spot of flame suddenly bloomed in the darkness. That flame shot into the air on a rising arc that carried it toward the open door leading into the loft.

Straight at Fargo.

He realized instantly what was happening. That was a flaming arrow coming at him, intended to land in the hayloft and set the barn on fire. That was exactly what would happen, too, if the arrow found its target. That dry hay would go up like tinder.

Fargo had only a second to react as the arrow sliced through the night air. He came up on his knees and lunged forward into the open doorway. Holding the rifle one-handed, he swung it through the air in front of him. He had to time the move perfectly. His nerves and muscles and eyes had to work together, because he would get only one chance at what he was trying to do.

The Henry's barrel hit the shaft of the arrow and knocked it aside. The arrow clattered against the barn wall only inches from the opening. Because Fargo had knocked it off its trajectory, it struck the wood at an angle and the flint head failed to penetrate. The arrow bounced off and fell to the ground in front of the barn, where the flames guttered out in the dirt.

The whole thing had happened so fast only a couple of heartbeats had gone by since the Comanche by the oaks fired the arrow. When he saw the arrow fall harmlessly to the ground, he let out an enraged squawk and reached for another arrow in the quiver slung on his back.

He never got it, because the slug from Fargo's rifle caught him in his still-open mouth, splintering his teeth, blasting through his upper spine, and exploding out the back of his neck. The warrior flopped backward and died.

Before the Comanche even hit the ground, Fargo had shifted his aim. He cranked off three swift shots at the figures running toward the cabin, firing as fast as he could work the Henry's lever. One of the Indians stumbled and then pitched forward on his face, but the other one kept going.

The dogs leaped at him, forcing him to slow down. The raider lifted his right arm. Starlight glinted on something in his hand, either a knife or a tomahawk. He was about to bring the weapon down on one of the dogs when another shot blasted, this time from the cabin. Muzzle flame spurted in a loophole that had been carved into the wall for just this purpose. The Indian staggered back, clutching his chest where the bullet had struck him, then fell as his knees folded up beneath him.

All three of the Comanches were down now. The problem was that they were just the vanguard of the attack. More figures ran from the trees and started to close in on the cabin.

Orange flashes winked in the darkness as shots rang out. From the sound of the reports, Fargo knew that most of them came from old muzzle-loaders, but those weapons could still be plenty deadly.

He knelt in the hayloft opening and started working the Henry again, spraying lead into the wave of attackers. Something whipped past his ear, and the next second an arrow embedded itself in the wall next to the door, only a foot away from him. As another arrow passed just over his head, he kicked backward, throwing himself out of the line of fire.

More shots came from both sides of the cabin. The Franklins were putting up a spirited defense of their home. Despite that, the Comanches were swarming around the place, and some of them had axes. The blades chopped into the shutters over the windows. If the raiders got inside, it would be a massacre.

Fargo stretched out on his belly to make himself a smaller target and thrust his rifle through the hayloft door again. He began firing, picking his shots. He had plenty of ammunition, but he didn't have time to just fire aimlessly into the attackers. There were so many of the Indians, he had to try to drop one with every round.

Four shots from the Trailsman sent four of the raiders spinning off their feet. But then two more flaming arrows sizzled through the night, and he couldn't stop them. They sailed over him and into the loft, burying themselves in the piles of hay. Instantly, more flames shot up as the dry stuff caught fire.

Fargo rolled over and surged to his feet. He couldn't put out the fire. It would spread too fast for that. The barn was doomed as soon as the first flaming arrow found its target. All he could do now was get the horses out of here, and get out himself.

Maybe the Comanches were after the horses more than anything else. Maybe if they got their hands on the animals, they would leave without wiping out everyone here. It was a slender hope, but better than no hope at all.

Fargo wasn't too worried about the Indians stealing the Ovaro. Any of them who tried would probably regret it. The stallion was a one-man horse, and a holy terror when he was angry.

The Trailsman grabbed his hat, clapped it on his head, and ran past the flames to the ladder. Despite the darkness, he went down it a lot faster than he had climbed up earlier in the night. When he reached the bottom, the horses were already neighing shrilly and slamming around in their stalls, spooked by the smoke that was spreading from the blaze in the loft.

Fargo hurried to the front doors, threw the bar aside, and then started opening the stalls. The horses bolted out and hit the doors in their panic, knocking them open, then stampeded across the open space between the barn and the cabin.

In their panic, the horses trampled several of the raiders who didn't have time to get out of the way. The Comanches' screams were cut short as steel-shod hooves pounded and slashed into them.

Fargo grabbed his saddle and flung it out of the barn. There were several other saddles sitting there, so he did the same with them. Then something nudged his shoulder, and he looked around to see the Ovaro behind him. The stallion lowered his head and bumped Fargo's shoulder again.

"I know. It's time to get out of here. Come on."

He picked up his rifle and took a step toward the doors, only to see them blocked suddenly. The fire in the loft was burning so furiously now that heat and smoke filled the barn, along with a garish red light. That hell-glow revealed the hate-twisted features of the two Comanche warriors who blocked Fargo's path.

One of them carried an old single-shot rifle. He swung it up toward Fargo. For close work like this, the Colt was faster and easier to use, so Fargo's right hand dropped to his side and palmed out the revolver with eye-blurring swiftness. His thumb looped over the hammer and drew it back as his finger tightened on the trigger. The Colt roared a split second before the Indian could fire.

The .44 slug punched into the Comanche's chest and drove him backward. His rifle went off as his finger spasmed on the trigger, but the barrel was pointed almost straight up as he fell.

The second warrior let out a howl of rage and flung the tomahawk he held at Fargo. Fargo had to twist aside from the weapon as it turned over and over in the air. That gave the Comanche time to tackle him.

Fargo went over backward with the warrior on top of him. His gun hand hit the ground hard enough to jolt the weapon out of his fingers. He still had the rifle in his other hand, but no room to bring it to bear.

The Comanche locked one hand around Fargo's throat and started trying to squeeze the life out of him. As a red haze slid over Fargo's vision, he reached down to his calf and drew the Arkansas toothpick from the sheath strapped there. He brought the knife up and buried the heavy razor-sharp blade in the Comanche's belly. The Indian shrieked in death-agony as the Trailsman ripped the knife to the side. Warm guts spilled out of the gaping wound.

Fargo shoved the dying Comanche aside. The walls of the barn were ablaze by now, and the roof was fully engulfed. It might collapse at any second. Fargo shoved the knife back in its sheath, grabbed the Colt he had dropped, and lunged to his feet. With the Ovaro beside him, he ran out of the barn. The burning roof came crashing down, barely missing them.

The stark illumination from the flames washed over the cabin as well. Fargo had no trouble seeing the Comanches now. Since the Colt was still in his hand, he used it, firing the four shots that remained in the cylinder. Three of the raiders went down.

He had personally accounted for a dozen of them, but there were at least twice that many still on their feet, trying to get into the cabin. Several of them succeeded, crashing through a window where they had chopped the shutters to pieces. Shots came from inside as the raiders started to climb through the opening, knocking one of the Indians back. But the others made it through, and Fargo heard screams from inside as he holstered his Colt and charged toward the cabin.

Before he could get there, Grace Franklin stepped out into the dogtrot from the other side of the cabin, leveled a shotgun at the Comanches, and let go with both barrels. Two of the warriors went down, shredded by the flying buckshot.

But there were too many of them. They filled the dogtrot, and one of them swung his rifle at Grace, catching her on the side of the head with the barrel. She fell, and Fargo couldn't see her anymore.

He hit the raiders from behind, slamming the butt of the Henry into one man's skull and feeling the satisfying crunch of bone shattering under the impact. He drew the Arkansas toothpick and lashed out right and left with it. Blood splattered hotly on his hand and face as he dealt out steely death at close quarters.

Something crashed against his head and sent him stumbling forward. He managed to stay on his feet and swung around, lashing out with the Henry and using it as a makeshift club. He bulled through the press of hostile bodies around him and found himself at the doorway of the other side of the cabin. It hung open, wrenched half off its hinges by the invaders. Fargo heard either Jessie or Emily scream again as he rushed in.

It was a scene from a madhouse inside the cabin. On one side of the room, Whit Franklin wrestled desperately with one of the raiders, trying to keep the Comanche from burying a knife in his chest. Jessie menaced another with a club that looked to be a leg broken off a chair. And Emily struggled frantically to escape the grip of two warriors who dragged her toward the window.

Fargo shot the Indian who was about to leap at Jessie with an upraised tomahawk. Then he swung toward Emily, intending to help free her from her captors. Before he could do so, one of the raiders landed on his back and drove him to his knees. The man grabbed his hair and jerked his head back. Fargo knew what came next—the keen edge of a knife slashing across his throat, spilling his life's blood on the puncheon floor.

He threw himself backward before the Comanche could cut his throat. They sprawled on the floor. Fargo rammed his elbow into the Comanche's belly and then writhed around to grab the man's wrist. He twisted hard enough that bone snapped and the Indian screeched in pain as the knife fell from his fingers.

Fargo snatched the weapon up by its bone handle and drove the blade deep into the Comanche's chest. The man arched his back in a dying spasm. Fargo rolled away from him and came up on hands and knees. He had dropped both the Colt and the Henry and couldn't locate them immediately. He saw Jessie running toward the window, though, screaming, "Emily! Emily!"

Emily and the two warriors were gone. Fargo had no doubt that the Comanches had succeeded in dragging the girl through the busted window.

He leaped to his feet and caught Jessie around the waist from behind. As he pulled her back, he shouted, "Stop it! If you go out there, they'll just get you, too!"

Jessie fought him. "Let me go! They took Emily! Let me go!"

Fargo looked around and saw that Whit was still on his feet. The Indian who'd been fighting with the young man now lay on the floor at Whit's feet, blood welling from the wound in his chest where Whit had turned his own knife against him.

The rest of the Comanches had fled from inside the cabin. Fargo shoved Jessie toward her brother. "Hang on to her! Don't let her go outside, whatever you do!"

He finally spotted his weapons and grabbed them from the floor. As he rushed out, he expected to find the dogtrot still full of Indians, but they were gone, including their dead and wounded. The only one in the dogtrot was Grace Franklin, who lay crumpled near the door of the other cabin.

Fargo wanted to check on her and see if she was still alive, but at the same time, he had to find out what had happened to Emily. As he ran out into the open area between the cabins and the burning barn, an arrow whipped past his head. He spotted a couple of warriors near the trees and jerked the Henry to his shoulder, but by the time he squeezed off a shot, they had ducked back into the shadows and disappeared.

In fact, *all* the Comanches were gone, except for the dead ones in the cabin. The rest of them had lit out for the tall and uncut, taking Emily with them.

Fargo's jaw tightened. The Comanches frequently took captives during their raids, so that was nothing unusual. They had probably gotten their hands on some of those horses Fargo had stampeded, and once they had a prisoner as well—and an attractive young woman, at that—they had decided that they'd paid a high enough price already and fled. Fargo was sure of it.

The Comanche were some of the finest horsemen in the world. This war party would have left their mounts somewhere close by, in the care of a couple of the younger warriors, and by now they would be mounted and galloping off into the night with Emily.

"Mr. Fargo? Where . . . where are they?"

Fargo turned to see that Whit had come up behind him. The young man's face was haggard with shock. He had bloodstains all over him from minor wounds he'd suffered during the fighting. Fargo started to ask where Jessie was, but then he spotted her in the dogtrot, kneeling next to her mother.

"They're gone. That's their way. Hit hard, and then run."

"And . . . and Emily?"

"They took her with them, I reckon."

Whit groaned. "Oh, Lord, no!" He grabbed Fargo's arm. "We've got to go after them!"

"I plan to. First, though, let's see how your ma's doing."

As they hurried into the dogtrot, Jessie looked up and said, "She's alive!"

Fargo dropped to a knee beside Grace. The light from the fire was enough to show him the welt on the side of her head where she had been struck down. It was already swollen and bruised but hadn't bled any. As far as Fargo could see, she didn't have any other wounds. Once she'd been knocked down, the Comanches had left her alone.

Grace let out a moan and started to stir. Jessie leaned over her and gripped her shoulders.

"Mama, can you hear me? Mama!"

Grace's eyes fluttered open. For a second, she seemed to have trouble focusing on anything. Then her gaze locked on Jessie's face, and she gasped.

"Jessie! You . . . you're all right?"

"I'm fine, Mama." Jessie's hair straggled in her face and she was pale from shock, but she didn't seem to be injured.

"Help me . . . sit up."

Fargo leaned forward to slip an arm around Grace's shoulders. He and Jessie lifted the older woman into a sitting position. Grace looked around. A look of fear came onto her face.

"My God, Whit, you're covered with blood!"

He shook his head. "Don't worry about me, Ma. A lot of it's not mine. I'm just scratched up a mite."

Grace's eyes were wide with panic, despite Whit's words. Her head jerked from side to side.

"Emily!" she said. "I don't see Emily!"

"The . . . the Comanches took her, Mama." Jessie had to force the words out.

Grace wailed and clapped her hands to her face. She swayed back and forth. She might have collapsed again if not for Fargo's strong arm around her shoulders.

"You have to go find her!" she managed to gasp out after a moment. "They can't have gone far."

"Chasing after them tonight is a good way to get Emily killed," Fargo said. "If they're pressed too hard, they'll just kill her and leave her behind to keep her from slowing them down."

Grace whimpered at the blunt but necessary words.

"That was a big war party," Fargo went on. "They won't be able to travel without leaving tracks that I can follow. I'll start after them first thing in the morning."

Grace clutched at his arm. "But . . . but what can you do? You're only one man."

Whit spoke up. "I'm going, too, Ma."

Fargo glanced at him, then back at Grace. "We'll talk about that in the morning. For now . . . Jessie, let's get your mother inside. She needs to lie down and rest. Whit, find a bucket and throw some water from the creek on the roof, to keep any sparks from landing on it and setting the cabin on fire."

"What about the barn?"

Fargo shook his head. "The barn's too far gone. You can't salvage any of it. Just let it burn down and keep the fire from spreading anywhere else."

Whit looked like he wanted to argue, but after a second he nodded and hurried off to do as Fargo said.

Fargo and Jessie helped Grace to her feet and into her side of the cabin. Jessie got her mother onto the four-poster bed, then turned to Fargo.

"I can handle this now, Mr. Fargo."

He nodded. "I'll go give Whit a hand. I need to see if there are any horses left around here, too."

He knew his Ovaro would be close by. The stallion would come when Fargo whistled. If he was going to set out after the war party that had taken Emily, though, he would probably need a packhorse and at least one extra mount.

Whit trotted back and forth from the creek, throwing bucketfuls of water onto the cabin roof. The barn continued to burn. A couple of the walls had fallen in already, and as Fargo paused to watch, another wall collapsed, sending sparks shooting high into the air. Fargo shook his head at the destruction, then dragged the saddles he had saved farther away from the flames. The heat was still intense, almost like a blow against the face.

Surprisingly, both dogs were still alive, although one of the big yellow curs limped as they trotted back and forth with Whit.

Fargo whistled, and sure enough, the Ovaro came trotting up out of the darkness almost right away. Fargo patted the big stallion's shoulder.

"You all right, old fella?" Fargo looked the Ovaro over

and was relieved when he didn't see any wounds or injuries.

The Ovaro would need to be in good shape if he was going to have any chance of finding Emily Franklin and bringing her back safely to her family.

4

It was a long night, what was left of it. Fargo saddled up the Ovaro and rode out to look for the other horses. He found four of them and drove them back to the ranch, where he picketed them near the cabin. Then he took over for a weary Whit and finished wetting down the cabin roof and the area around it.

Exhaustion and shock had overwhelmed Grace Franklin. She was asleep, with Jessie sitting in a rocking chair she had pulled over beside the bed. One of the lamps was lit but turned down low. When Fargo stuck his head in the door to check on them, Jessie stood up and came over to him, motioning for him to step back out into the dogtrot.

Jessie joined him, easing the door closed behind her. "Mama's resting. That's the best thing for her right now, I think."

Fargo nodded. "I agree. Maybe you should try to get some sleep, too."

Jessie's reaction was an emphatic shake of her head. "I can't do that. Not as long as Emily is out there somewhere, a prisoner of those savages."

"I'm going after them. I'll find her and bring her back."

"Not before they've had a chance to brutalize her."

Fargo didn't say anything. They both knew what was likely to happen to Emily while she was a captive.

"Whit's bound and determined to go with you, you know," Jessie went on after a moment.

"I know. I'm not sure it's a good idea, though."

"Then you're *really* not going to like what I'm about to say next. I want to come along, too."

Fargo frowned. "That's impossible."

"Why? Whit admitted I can ride better than he can, and Emily was right about me being a better shot, too. I can help you just as much as Whit, maybe more."

"Somebody's going to need to stay here to take care of your mother."

"I was thinking we could take her to town. We have friends there she could stay with—"

"That would take an extra couple of days before we actually got on the trail of those Comanches. Two more days Emily would have to be a captive."

Jessie sighed. "Damn it . . . you're right. I know that. But I feel like I have to do *something*."

"Take care of your mother and the ranch. That's how you'll help."

"I'm not worried about the ranch. The Indians can have the rest of the cattle and horses, as far as I'm concerned. They're not likely to come back anytime soon, though, are they? After raiding the place like they did tonight?"

Fargo had to admit that she had a point. "But it'll still be best if you stay here."

Jessie gave up the argument. "All right. What about Whit?"

"He can come along, I reckon. As long as he doesn't slow me down. I found enough horses so that we can take along an extra saddle mount and a pack animal. We'll need to put together some supplies . . ."

Jessie nodded. "I can do that. I'll start on it right now, in fact, so that you can ride out as soon as it's light enough."

Fargo smiled. "Good idea. I'll tell Whit."

The young man was excited by the news. "I'll get my rifle and six-gun." He started toward the cabin.

"Hold on. We're not leaving for a while yet. Why don't you try to get a little sleep instead? I'll wake you up in plenty of time."

Whit looked doubtful. "I don't know. I'm not sure I could sleep right now, as upset as I am about Emily."

"You'll be more alert tomorrow, and better able to give me a hand if I need it."

"Well . . . in that case, I reckon I can give it a try. But I'm still not sure I'll be able to sleep."

Fargo stuck his head in that side of the cabin ten minutes later. Loud snores came from the sleeping loft where Whit had his bed. Fargo chuckled at the sound.

There were rocking chairs in this cabin, too. He sat down in one of them, leaned back, and tipped his hat forward over his eyes. He fell almost instantly into a light sleep, but a part of his brain remained aware and alert. That catlike slumber allowed him to rest, but he could be fully awake at a second's notice, if need be.

Sometime later, his eyes snapped open. Gray light that heralded the approach of dawn came in through the window with the broken shutters. The faint illumination showed him that Jessie had come over to this side of the cabin and sat down on the floor beside the rocking chair. She leaned against Fargo's leg, pillowing her head on his thigh. She wasn't moving, and her deep, regular breathing told Fargo that she was asleep.

He smiled in the early-morning gloom. His hand moved, stroked Jessie's golden hair for a second. She shifted slightly but didn't awaken. Fargo sat there, breathing deeply himself, drawing strength from Jessie's companionship as well as from the cool air. During a Texas summer, the predawn hours like this were about the only time the air was cool.

Unfortunately, today the air was filled as well with the smell of ashes from the barn, a vivid reminder of the destruction that the raiding Comanches had carried out.

That stirred Fargo to action. He sat up, and the movement was enough to rouse Jessie from sleep. She looked flustered and embarrassed as she moved away from his leg.

"I'm sorry. I just . . . I just got so tired, and my mother was sleeping soundly, and I thought I'd just rest for a few minutes . . ."

Fargo refrained from pointing out that she could have slept in the rocking chair on the other side of the cabin if she'd wanted to. Jessie had wanted company, and Fargo certainly didn't mind.

There were practical matters to consider. "Did you get those supplies packed up?" he asked her.

"Yes. Luckily, we'd just been to Weatherford, so we had plenty of everything on hand. Sugar and flour and beans, some salt pork . . ."

Fargo nodded. "That'll be fine. We might be able to get some fresh meat along the way, too."

Jessie stood up and brushed herself off after sitting on the floor. She ran her fingers through her hair.

"Land's sake, I must look a sight. But that doesn't matter now, does it?"

Fargo got to his feet as well. "I'll go check on the horses." He jerked a thumb toward the loft, where Whit was still sawing wood. "Better wake up your brother, too, and then start some coffee boiling."

He went out into the early morning. The Ovaro was by the creek, cropping grass that grew on the bank. Fargo hadn't picketed the stallion. He knew the Ovaro wasn't going to wander off. The stallion saw him and tossed his head in greeting.

The dogs ran around Fargo's legs. He patted both of them and scratched their ears, then took a look at the horses he had rounded up to make sure none of them had been wounded in the fighting. The only injuries he found were some scratches from the brush they had run through as they were bolting away from the fire. He had some dope in his saddlebags that he would daub on them later to keep the scratches from festering.

Whit came out of the cabin, yawning and scratching his belly and running the fingers of his other hand through his rumpled hair. "Ready to ride?" he asked.

"We'll have some breakfast first. It may be a while before we get a chance to have a real meal again."

The smell of coffee brewing and bacon frying soon filled

the cabin. Fargo inhaled deeply and appreciatively as he came in with Whit.

Grace Franklin was sitting up on the bed. She put a hand to her head and winced in pain, then looked at Fargo.

"I hoped for a second when I woke up that it was all just a terrible nightmare, but it isn't, is it?"

Fargo shook his head. "I'm afraid not."

"Emily really is gone."

"But we're gonna get her back, Ma," Whit said. "Mr. Fargo and I are leavin' in just a few minutes to get on the trail of those Indians."

Grace swung her legs off the bed and stood up. She swayed and clutched one of the posts at the foot of the bed. Fargo put a hand on her arm to steady her as well.

"Whit, you're just a boy! You can't—"

"I'm a grown man, Ma. I'm a good rider and a good shot, and Mr. Fargo doesn't need to be goin' after those savages alone. I can help him find Emily and bring her home."

Jessie had hotcakes and bacon frying in a big, cast-iron skillet at the fireplace. She said, "We'll stay here and take care of the ranch, Mama." She didn't sound particularly happy about it.

"The hell with the ranch!" Jessie and Whit looked startled at their mother's vehement exclamation. "I want my little girl back!"

Fargo patted her arm. "We'll do everything we can."

Grace sank back on the edge of the bed, covered her face with her hands, and began to sob. Jessie and Whit looked stricken and upset, but helpless to do anything that might make Grace feel better.

"Just finish fixing breakfast," Fargo told Jessie.

Grace refused to eat when the food was ready. Fargo advised Jessie not to try to force her mother to eat. Even though Fargo was still sore and tired, with eyes gritty from lack of real sleep, he felt human again after he had washed down a big plate of hotcakes and bacon with two cups of strong black coffee.

The gray light was taking on a slight rosy hue when Fargo stepped out of the cabin to see to it that the horses were saddled and ready to go. He left Whit inside to say good-bye to his mother and sister.

Whit came out a few minutes later, followed by Jessie. Each of them carried a bag of supplies. Fargo took the bags and tied them onto the horse he had picked out for a pack animal. He had saddled the other two horses they would be taking with them, one for Whit . . .

And the other for Emily to ride once they had rescued her.

"Be careful," Fargo told Jessie. "Keep your eyes open while we're gone. I don't think that war party will come back, but you can't ever be sure about things like that."

Jessie nodded. "How long do you think you'll be gone?"

"Just a few days, I hope."

"But it could be longer?"

"It could," Fargo said. He wasn't going to lie to her. If he and Whit had to pursue the Indians deep into Comancheria, as the land to the northwest was sometimes called, it could be weeks before they returned.

Assuming, of course, that they made it back alive.

Jessie stepped closer to Fargo and put her arms around him, pressing her body to his. "Be careful, Skye," she said in a whisper. "Come back safe, and bring Emily with you."

Fargo nodded. He kissed the top of Jessie's head, aware that Whit was watching but not particularly caring at the moment.

She stepped back and then hugged Whit, too. In a gruff voice, he said, "Don't worry. We'll be fine. And we'll bring Emily back, too. Those blasted Comanch' won't know what hit 'em."

Jessie summoned up a smile. "That's right."

Fargo and Whit swung up into their saddles. Fargo handed the reins of the extra mount to Whit and took the packhorse's reins himself. He lifted a hand in farewell as they turned the horses and rode out.

"My sister's sweet on you, you know," Whit said when they were out of easy earshot of the cabin.

"I reckon she's more worried about Emily right now than anything else."

"Yeah, but she's still sweet on you, Mr. Fargo." Whit laughed. "And you don't know just how stubborn my sister can be when it comes to getting what she wants."

Fargo just smiled and shook his head.

He knew the Indians had headed northwest, and it took only a few minutes to find the tracks of their unshod ponies leading in that direction. Fargo knew the war party still numbered at least two dozen. Getting Emily away from them without getting him and Whit killed in the process was going to be tricky.

Luckily, Fargo could be as sneaky as a Comanche himself. He planned to follow the war party until they caught up, then slip into the Indians' camp and free Emily without the Comanches knowing what was going on. If he could do that, then it would be a race back to Lost Valley—assuming the raiders gave chase. They might not deem one prisoner worthy of going to that much trouble.

But he was getting ahead of himself with those thoughts, Fargo knew. For now, as the sun began to peek over the horizon, he concentrated on following the tracks left by their quarry. That wasn't too difficult, since the Comanches hadn't been trying to hide their trail.

Why would they? They were headed into a land where most men wouldn't dare follow them.

Unfortunately for the Comanches, Skye Fargo wasn't most men.

The Indians hadn't taken any pains to conceal their tracks, but they had been moving fast and they had probably traveled all night. That meant they had a big lead on Fargo and Whit. They would slow down in a day or two, though, once they figured they were out of danger. That was when the two pursuers would have to make up some ground. Fargo warned

Whit that they were facing some long, hard days in the saddle.

"That's all right. Whatever it takes to get Emily back is fine with me, Mr. Fargo. But will the horses hold up to a pace like that?"

"This stallion of mine will," Fargo said. "I don't know about the others. They look like fine specimens of horseflesh, but you'd know better than I would how much sand they have."

"Plenty, I think. We've had good luck with our breeding stock."

"We'll stop and rest them as often as we have to. You can switch out and ride that other saddle mount some of the time, too. We need to keep them as fresh as we can, because once we have Emily, we may need to make a run for it."

Fargo's prediction was accurate. He and Whit spent long, tiring hours in the saddle that day, and by late afternoon, Whit was showing signs of discouragement because they didn't seem to be any closer to the Indians than they had been when they started that morning.

"You said it yourself the last time you checked the droppings their horses left, Mr. Fargo. They're still five or six hours ahead of us, at least. And we're gonna have to stop when it gets dark, aren't we?"

Fargo nodded. "There won't be enough of a moon to let us keep trailing them at night. Too easy to lose the trail that way, and then we'd just fall even farther behind. I've gone after Indian captives before, Whit. You have to be patient on a job like this."

"Hard to do when you know what's happening to your sister." Whit's voice was choked with emotion as he spoke.

"What's important is getting Emily back alive. Nothing else. You just hold on to that thought."

Whit swallowed hard and nodded. "All right. But it ain't easy."

"Not many things in life are," Fargo said.

They were still in the range of rugged hills that stretched

northwestward from Lost Valley, but Fargo knew they would reach flatter terrain the next day. He had been through this country before. The slopes became long and gentle. An occasional mesa dotted the mostly level landscape. It was a big, empty country. If they kept going long enough, they would come to the area watered by the Double Mountain Forks of the Brazos, where several Comanche bands had their hunting grounds. That was the heart of Comancheria, a place where a white man's life wasn't worth a plugged nickel.

Fargo and Whit kept moving until it was almost too dark to see the trail, then found a place to camp for the night. Fargo decided on a small clearing in some trees, next to a rock that jutted some twenty feet in the air. He built a small fire at the base of that rock, where it couldn't be seen for miles around as it might have if they camped out in the open. Their midday meal had consisted of some of the hotcakes left over from that morning's breakfast, washed down with water from their canteens. Whit was eager for some hot food and coffee and said as much.

"Take care of the other horses," Fargo told him. "I'll tend to my stallion. He's a mite skittish when other folks try to mess with him."

"I'll keep that in mind. He looks like he wouldn't mind takin' a bite out of my hide."

Fargo chuckled. "Don't tempt him, or he's liable to do it."

After they had eaten, Fargo cleaned the coffeepot and frying pan with sand and put out the fire. "Are we gonna take turns standin' guard?" Whit asked.

Fargo shook his head. "I don't reckon that's necessary. We both need some rest, and that horse of mine will let us know if anybody comes skulking around. He's better than any watchdog I've ever seen."

A surprised frown came over Whit's face. "Are you sure? I figured we'd need to keep an eye out for other Comanches."

"That war party traveling through will have scattered any

smaller bands. Sort of like how all the other birds will leave the area when a big hawk comes cruising along."

"Oh. All right. If you say so, Mr. Fargo. You're the Trailsman, after all."

Fargo smiled. "Call me Skye. We're partners now."

Whit looked pleased by that idea. "Sure, Skye."

"I'll just take a quick look around. You go ahead and spread your bedroll. Get some sleep, Whit. Tomorrow will be another long day."

Whit spread his blankets and rolled up in them while Fargo took his rifle and walked out about a hundred yards from the camp, then made a circuit around the place. When he came back a few minutes later, he shook out his blankets, moved his saddle a little so that it was in a better position for him to use it as a pillow, then stretched out and wrapped the blankets around him. Night had fallen. The stars were out, a sliver of moon hung low in the sky, and the camp was quiet and still.

At least until Whit started to snore again.

"How long are we gonna wait before we kill them bastards? I thought Fargo was gonna stumble right over us while he was walkin' around!"

Martin's voice was a soft whisper that no one could hear more than a few feet away. He and Sabin and Jackson lay in the shadows under the trees, staring through the darkness toward the spot where Fargo and Whit Franklin had made camp.

"Take it easy, Martin." Sabin had to work to keep his naturally rumbling voice down. "I want to make sure they're good and asleep before we move in. We'll ventilate 'em and then get the hell outta here."

"That can't be too soon to suit me," Jackson said. "I don't like being on this side of the Brazos."

"Neither do I. But I got a score to settle with that son of a bitch Fargo, and I ain't goin' back until he's dead."

Sabin hadn't known exactly where the Franklin ranch was,

but after he'd paid his fine for disturbing the peace and the judge had turned him loose, he had asked around Weatherford until he found somebody who could tell him about Lost Valley and how to get there. The same person confirmed that Fargo had left town with the Franklins.

Sabin wasn't going back to his job or doing anything else until he caught up to the man who had humiliated him not once but twice. The man who would have to pay for that with his life.

Skye Fargo.

When the three of them approached the ranch, though, they had seen right away that something terrible had happened here. The barn was a pile of smoldering rubble. Sabin, Martin, and Jackson had spent enough time on the frontier to recognize the signs of an Indian raid when they saw them. They didn't know if anybody was still alive down there. But in reconnoitering around the ranch, they had found the tracks of several shod horses heading northwest, following the trail of a large group of Indian ponies.

That was all Sabin needed to see. He was convinced that Fargo was one of the men who'd gone after the Comanches. He had declared that *they* were going after Fargo, and after some whining from Martin and a few grumbled complaints from Jackson, the two of them had gone along with the idea.

Perhaps foolishly, they had almost ridden their horses into the ground. Sabin had pushed them at a hard pace all day. But now that effort was going to pay off, because they had caught up while there was still barely enough light in the sky to recognize Fargo and Whit Franklin as the two men ate their supper and then curled up in their blankets. They were sleeping now . . .

And if Sabin had his way, they would never wake up.

More time went by. A slender slice of moon rose higher in the heavens. Finally, Sabin nodded and gripped his rifle tighter.

"All right. It's time."

He stood up. The other two followed suit. With surprising stealth for such a big man, Sabin stole forward. Martin and

Jackson were right behind him, also clutching rifles. The three men reached the edge of the trees and paused, raising their weapons.

"Now!" Sabin said, and the rifles poised, ready to deal out flaming death.

5

Fargo heard a faint crackle of brush, the soft scrape of boot leather on the ground, and rose up on his knees on the rock that loomed over the campsite. His keen eyes spotted the figures of three men as they stepped out from the shelter of the trees. He snugged the butt of the Henry against his shoulder and waited until they lifted their own rifles to carry out what amounted to a cold-blooded execution.

Then he stroked the Henry's trigger just as Sabin said, "Now!"

Muzzle flame lanced from the rifle's barrel as Fargo fired. Sabin was easy to distinguish because he was so much bigger than the other two. Fargo aimed his first shot at the big mule skinner's chest. As the smashing impact of the slug rocked Sabin back on his heels, Fargo was already levering another round into the Henry's firing chamber and shifting his aim. He snapped a shot at the man on Sabin's left, then pivoted smoothly and fired at the one to Sabin's right. Both men dropped their rifles and went down.

Sabin was still on his feet, though, roaring now in pain and outrage. Fargo shouted, "Stay down, Whit!" and cranked another round into the Henry as Sabin tilted his rifle toward the top of the rock. The two shots came so close together they sounded like one. Fargo felt as much as heard the wind-rip of Sabin's bullet as it passed close beside his ear.

Hit again, Sabin twisted halfway around and fell to his knees. Fargo levered the Henry and fired again. This time, the slug hammered Sabin all the way to the ground. Fargo lowered the rifle and peered over its barrel. Sabin wasn't moving now. He was a motionless black hulk.

"Whit! Are you all right?" Fargo knew the young man should be unharmed, since the only shot any of the three men had gotten off was the one Sabin had loosed at him. That bullet hadn't missed by much, but close wasn't good enough in a gunfight.

Whit's voice had a stunned quality to it when he answered. "Y-yeah, I . . . I guess so. Skye . . . where are you? What just happened?"

"Get your gun and cover those three varmints. I'll be down in a minute."

Fargo climbed down the far side of the rock and circled back around to the camp. As he walked up, Whit turned quickly toward him. The young man had gotten out of his bedroll and stood there holding his rifle.

"Take it easy, Whit. It's just me."

"But . . . but I thought you were asleep, like me!"

Fargo gestured toward the sprawled bodies. "So did they. But I slipped out of my blankets earlier and got on top of that rock while they were still sneaking up on the camp. I knew they were out there, and I had a hunch they intended to bushwhack us."

"You knew? How did you know?"

"Had a feeling that someone was trailing us. My gut told me that we were being watched, and I've learned to trust my instincts. I felt the same way when we were traveling between Weatherford and Lost Valley, and I'm convinced it was the Comanches keeping an eye on us then. They were waiting for us to get back to the ranch before they attacked."

"I reckon you must be right. You know a lot more about this sort of thing than I do." Whit shook his head. "I didn't even have any idea somebody was following us."

"I was sure of it once I'd taken a look around. They thought I didn't know where they were hiding in the brush, but I did. Go ahead and start getting your gear together. We'll need to find another camp."

"Why do we have to do that?"

Fargo turned toward the horses. "Those shots could be heard a long way off. We don't want to be sitting here if anybody gets curious and comes to see what they were about."

"Oh. Like more Indians, you mean."

"That's exactly what I—"

Fargo stopped short as he caught a flicker of motion in the corner of his eye. As he wheeled around, he saw one of Sabin's companions, the fox-faced hombre called Martin, pushing himself up from the ground with a gun in his hand. In a moment of unaccustomed carelessness, Fargo had failed to make sure all three men were dead.

He might pay for that mistake with his life, because as fast as he was, it was hard to outdraw a gun that was already drawn. Fargo's hand stabbed toward his Colt anyway.

The roar of another gunshot split the night. Martin pitched forward to sprawl on his face. His gun slipped unfired from his fingers.

Fargo had cleared leather, but his gun still pointed downward. He brought it up as another figure stepped out of the shadows underneath the trees, powder smoke curling from the barrel of the rifle in its hands. Fargo trained his Colt on the dark shape. Whoever it was might have just saved his life, but that didn't mean Fargo was ready to trust him.

"Hold it right there."

"It's me, Skye."

Fargo stiffened in surprise as he recognized the voice. He wasn't the only one. Whit said, "Jessie! What in blazes are you doing here?"

She laughed softly as she stepped forward. "Saving your bacon, from the looks of it." She came to a stop in front of Fargo. "It's a good thing I'm stubborn as a mule, isn't it?"

Fargo couldn't help but chuckle. "I reckon so. Better move aside right now, though. I need to make sure all three of those hombres are dead. We don't want any *more* surprises tonight."

* * *

An hour later, they had moved to another camp on top of a hill more than a mile away from the spot where the shootout with Sabin and the other two had taken place. It was a cold camp, with no fire to attract any more attention than the gunshots may have already.

They had left the bodies of Sabin, Martin, and Jackson behind for the scavengers, a decision that obviously made Jessie and Whit a little uncomfortable. Fargo wasn't going to take the time or trouble to bury three bushwhacking bastards, though. It was more important that they get moving as quickly as possible.

He didn't even delay long enough to ask Jessie what she was doing there. Now, though, after they had unsaddled the horses, it was time to get an answer to that question.

"You were supposed to stay at the ranch and take care of your mother," Fargo said.

"Yeah, you didn't leave Ma there alone, did you?" Whit wanted to know.

Jessie shook her head. There was enough light from the moon and stars now that the three of them could see one another.

"The Bradshaws showed up not long after the two of you left. They offered to take her back to their place and look after her and the ranch until we get back with Emily."

"Who are the Bradshaws?" Fargo asked.

"A family that lives just over the river. They have the westernmost spread in those parts, except for ours. They saw the glow from the fire in the sky last night and knew something must be wrong. Clinton Bradshaw and all seven of his sons showed up, armed for trouble."

Whit said, "You should have gone back to their place with them, Jessie."

"I figured I could be more help coming after you and Skye." Her chin tilted in defiance. "I was right, too. Martin might have killed both of you."

"So you took the other horse and followed our trail?" Fargo said.

Jessie shrugged. "It wasn't that hard. And obviously, I

wasn't the only one. I guess Sabin and the others were behind me. I made camp about half a mile behind you. The three of them must have passed me and never knew I was there. I was hidden in some pretty thick brush. Then when I heard all the shooting, I figured I'd better come see what had happened." She hesitated. "I was afraid that both of you . . . well, that you might be dead. I don't know what I would have done then. Tried to pick off Sabin and the others one by one, I guess."

"And gotten yourself killed, too," Whit said. "Damn it, Jessie—"

"Look, I'm here, and I'm not going back. You might as well stop acting like my big brother and accept that, Whit."

"But I *am* your big brother."

"And the three of us will stand a better chance of rescuing Emily. Isn't that right, Skye?"

Fargo chuckled. "Don't get me in the middle of an argument between a brother and sister."

"But you're not going to try to send me back, are you?"

Fargo shook his head. "No, I don't reckon I am."

Whit started to protest. "But, Skye—"

"Jessie will be safer with us than she would be traveling all the way back to the Brazos by herself. And if she's as good a shot as she claims she is, she may come in handy."

Jessie smiled. "I am. You'll see."

"More than likely," Fargo said. "Because somebody's bound to try to kill us again."

By morning, Whit still wasn't happy about Jessie coming along with them, but he didn't say much. The rest of the night had passed quietly, with Fargo and Whit taking turns standing guard, and at first light the three of them mounted up and rode northwestward, following the tracks left by the Comanche war party.

After a while, Whit said, "You used me as bait last night, didn't you, Skye?"

"I was trying to draw Sabin and the others out into the open, so I reckon you could say that."

"What if they had shot me?"

Fargo smiled. "I didn't plan on letting that happen. But maybe I should have let you in on what I was doing. I just figured it would be best if everything looked natural, like we didn't suspect anything."

After a moment, Whit gave a grudging nod. "That makes sense. But I still don't have to like it."

"No, I don't suppose you do."

"I don't like Jessie being along, either."

She smiled at him. "Well, that's just too bad, Whit."

Fargo nudged the Ovaro a short distance ahead of the other two. If they were going to start squabbling again, he didn't want to have to listen to it.

By midmorning, they were out of the hills and into the flatter country that Fargo was expecting. If anything, the tracks were even easier to follow now. The Comanches weren't worried about anybody trailing them up here into their stronghold.

They weren't moving quite as fast, either. Fargo estimated the war party was only about four hours ahead now.

When he mentioned that, Whit got an eager look on his face. "Then we can catch up to them today."

Fargo nodded. "If you want to warn them that we're on their trail."

Whit frowned and shook his head. "What do you mean?"

"We're not kicking up much dust, but enough for them to see us if we crowd them too close. We need to wait until tonight, when they've made camp again, and then close in on them."

"How do you plan to get Emily away from them?" Jessie asked.

Fargo ran a thumbnail along his bearded jaw. "I've been giving that some thought. I'll have to slip into their camp and bring her out. That won't be easy, but I think I can do it. Then we'll light a shuck for home and put as much distance as we can between us and them, as fast as we can."

Whit looked worried. "But what if they come after us?"

"That's what I've been pondering, some way to slow them

down. I was thinking maybe the two of you could flank out and start a couple of prairie fires if I give you the signal. The wind's out of the south, so it would carry the flames toward the Comanche camp, and if the two fires burned together to make one big blaze, the war party would have to go all the way around to come after us. That would give us a good start." Fargo shrugged. "But we'll have to wait and see how everything plays out. That may not work."

"Whatever you need us to do, we'll do," Jessie said. "We just want to get Emily back."

"We agree on that," Whit said with a nod.

They rode on. After another hour or so, Whit suddenly stiffened in his saddle and pointed off to the southwest.

"Look yonder. There's some dust, Skye. Is it coming from the war party?"

Fargo shook his head. "Not unless they've backtracked and gone an awful long way around to get where they're going. I think the Comanches we're after are still somewhere ahead of us. That dust is coming from somebody else."

"Who?" Jessie asked.

"More Comanches?" Fargo suggested with a tight-lipped smile.

"What are we going to do?" Whit asked. "It looks like the dust is movin' in this direction."

"It is. I've been keeping an eye on it for a while."

Whit's eyes narrowed. "You already knew somebody was out there, comin' toward us?"

"That's right."

"You're in the habit of keepin' things to yourself, aren't you?"

"I say what I need to when the time comes." Fargo reined in and pointed to a small mesa about half a mile away. "We'll ride over there and put that mesa between us and whoever that is. That way, they won't know we're anywhere around unless we want them to."

He nudged the Ovaro into motion again. Whit and Jessie followed him toward the mesa, which rose about forty feet from the plains around it. The sides looked sheer from a distance, but when the three riders got closer, Fargo saw that the elements had worn a number of seams into them.

"I think I can get up there and take a look." He reached into his saddlebags and brought out a pair of field glasses, then swung down.

"You want me to come with you?" Whit asked.

"No, it'll be better if you stay here."

Fargo studied the cracks in the side of the mesa for a moment and then decided which one looked like it would be the easiest to climb. Hanging the field glasses around his neck by their rawhide strap, he began pulling himself up, testing each foothold and handhold before trusting his weight to it.

It took him only a few minutes to climb to the top of the mesa, which was about fifty yards in diameter, its flat top tufted with hardy grass and dotted with clumps of rocks. He went to the far side of it and knelt there, lifting the field glasses to his eyes. The cloud of dust was half a mile away, he estimated. He peered through the glasses at the base of the cloud in an attempt to make out the riders causing it.

Fargo stiffened in surprise as he saw blue uniforms and a guidon whipping in the breeze. That was a cavalry patrol about to cut across the trail of the Comanches who had stolen Emily Franklin from her home. He counted twenty troopers with an officer and a noncom leading them.

He didn't know if those cavalrymen were looking for the war party or were just out on a routine patrol. They had to have come from Fort Griffin. The real question in Fargo's mind was whether to let them go past or try to intercept them.

He didn't have to ponder that for very long. The best way to rescue Emily was still for him to slip into the Indians' camp and steal her back from them, but having the cavalry along might make all the difference in the world in whether or not they got away safely. Chances were, the Comanches wouldn't risk taking on the patrol for the sake of one captive and would flee deeper into Comancheria instead.

With that thought in mind, Fargo hurried back over to the place where he had climbed to the top of the mesa and looked down at Whit and Jessie, who had their heads tilted back to watch for him.

Fargo waved an arm toward the riders in the distance. "It's the cavalry! Ride out there and meet them!"

Whit gave an excited nod and turned his horse. Jessie stayed where she was, though, while Fargo climbed back down to the ground.

Fargo caught up the stallion's reins and swung into the saddle. "Why didn't you go with Whit?"

"I wanted to stay and ride with you."

Fargo put the Ovaro into motion. He led the spare saddle mount while Jessie cantered along beside him. Whit had taken the pack animal with him. Fargo looked ahead and saw that the patrol was close enough now to make out the blue uniforms without the field glasses. Whit was moving straight toward them. The cavalrymen slowed.

"Will this help us get Emily back?" Jessie asked.

"It should. Having the cavalry along will come close enough to evening up the odds that the Comanches probably won't chase after us once we get her away from them."

"You think they'll just turn her over to us?"

Fargo shook his head. "No, we'll still have to do like we planned. I'll have to go into their camp and get her. If they spot those troopers before then, they'll kill her for sure and leave her body for us to find."

A shudder went through Jessie. "You're a plainspoken man, aren't you, Skye?"

"I've found that anything else is a waste of time."

"Well, in that case . . ." Jessie looked over at him. "I find you very attractive, Skye Fargo. I hope that sometime I get a chance to show you just how much." She grinned. "Is that plainspoken enough for you?"

Fargo returned the grin. "I reckon it is. And I feel pretty much the same way about you."

"I'm awful for even thinking about such a thing while Emily's being held prisoner by those savages, aren't I?"

"Not really. Folks generally feel the same sort of yearnings no matter what the circumstances. Sometimes they just can't do anything about 'em, that's all."

"We'll have to wait and see what happens, won't we?"

"Yep."

By now, Whit had met up with the cavalry patrol, which had come to a stop. As Fargo and Jessie rode up, the officer in charge spurred his horse over to meet them.

"Mr. Fargo? I'm Lieutenant Hamilton Kemp. Very pleased to meet you."

Lt. Kemp extended a hand. Fargo shook it and gave the officer a nod. "Lieutenant Kemp."

"I've heard about you, of course, and the scouting work that you've done for the army. The young man tells me that you're after a white captive taken by the Comanche? His sister, I believe?"

"That's right." Fargo inclined his head toward Jessie. "This is Miss Jessie Franklin, the other sister."

Kemp tugged on the brim of his campaign cap. "Miss Franklin. It's an honor and a privilege."

"Thank you, Lieutenant. Can you help us get Emily back from those savages?"

Kemp frowned. He was on the smallish size and young, no more than thirty. He had sleek dark hair and a neatly trimmed beard.

"The mission with which we're charged isn't really about rescuing captives, miss. My superiors at Fort Griffin have received reports of Comanche raiding parties venturing down into the area around Weatherford. Our orders are to locate those parties and engage them if circumstances are such as to make a successful engagement possible. Otherwise, we are to reconnoiter the area and establish a sense of how strong the hostiles' forces really are."

Jessie frowned. "Is that your way of saying that you *won't* help us?"

"Not at all. Simply that retrieving white captives isn't the highest priority for this troop of cavalry."

"You won't have to retrieve Emily Franklin, Lieutenant,"

Fargo said. "I'll do that. We just need you around to persuade the Comanches they'd be better off not coming after us."

Kemp shook his head. "Oh, no, I can't permit that."

Fargo frowned. "Can't permit what?"

"I can't allow civilians to interact with the hostiles. That's strictly the responsibility of the military." Kemp smiled. "No, Mr. Fargo, since you're not working for the army at the present time, I'm afraid I have no choice but to order you to turn around and return to Weatherford . . . and take Mr. and Miss Franklin with you."

6

Fargo's eyes narrowed to angry slits. Even under the best of circumstances, he didn't like anybody bossing him around. He liked it even less when the orders came from some wet-behind-the-ears junior officer with an inflated opinion of his own importance.

"You said it yourself, Lieutenant. We're civilians. You don't have the authority to order us to turn around and go back."

"Oh, but I do." Kemp still wore a smug, infuriating smile. "We're beyond the reach of any state, county, or local authorities out here, Mr. Fargo. The army is the only authority that *does* have any jurisdiction beyond the westernmost edge of the frontier."

"You couldn't make that stick in a court of law."

"I don't see a judge and a bailiff out here, do you?"

As Fargo's jaw tightened, the burly noncom accompanying the patrol rode over to join the little group. He had sergeant's stripes on his sleeves, which were rolled up over brawny, sunburned forearms. His broad face was also sunburned. Fair hair poked out from under his campaign cap. His eyes moved boldly over Jessie before setting on Fargo and narrowing in a glare.

"Got a problem here, Lieutenant?"

"No problem, Sergeant. I was just explaining to this gentleman that it will be impossible for him and his companions to continue their pursuit of the hostiles. This is Skye Fargo, by the way. Mr. Fargo, Sergeant Pike Monroe."

The sergeant grunted in recognition but didn't look any

friendlier. "The Trailsman, eh? I've heard plenty about you, mister. Never believed half of it, myself."

"No offense, Sergeant, but I don't care what you believe." Fargo turned back to Kemp. "Lieutenant, just how do you intend to rescue Emily from the Comanches?"

"I told you, that's not our mission." Kemp was starting to look and sound a little annoyed. "But from what the young man told me, the war party is of a comparable size to our patrol, so I see no reason not to catch up to them and engage them. The young lady will be freed once we've defeated the hostiles."

Fargo's face was grim. "That's what I was afraid you'd say. The young lady will be *dead* if you jump that war party, Lieutenant. They'll cut her throat as soon as they hear your bugler blowing the charge."

"You seem awfully certain of that."

"I've fought Indians before. Have you?"

The flush that appeared on Kemp's face told Fargo the answer to that question. The young officer was inexperienced and eager for something to put on his record— like a battle with the Comanches.

Sgt. Monroe edged his mount forward. "Listen here, Fargo. *I've* fought Injuns before, plenty of times, and I say the lieutenant's right. We've got our orders, blast it. We can't ignore them because of some gal who was unlucky enough to get carried off."

Whit had ridden over to join them while they were talking. Now he spoke up angrily. "Emily's not just some gal. She's my sister, and if Mr. Fargo knows a better way of getting her back, you ought to listen to him."

Monroe sneered at him. "And why should we do that, kid? You three are just civilians. You ain't the bosses out here."

Kemp held up a hand. "Take it easy, Sergeant. We've gotten off on the wrong foot here." He turned to Whit and Jessie. "I promise you that we'll do everything in our power to free your sister from the hostiles. But we have to proceed according to our orders and carry out our mission in proper military fashion."

"No matter what happens to Emily," Whit said.

Before Kemp could respond to that, Jessie spoke up. "I understand, Lieutenant." She ignored the angry glance that Whit shot in her direction. "But I was wondering if I could ask one favor of you."

Kemp smiled. "Of course. I can't guarantee that I can carry out your wishes, though."

"Instead of sending us back, couldn't we come along with you?" When Kemp frowned and opened his mouth to respond, Jessie hurried on before he could say anything. "I don't mean that we'd take part in your action against the Comanches, of course. We're just civilians. But we could wait out of harm's way while you engage the war party, and then when you've freed Emily, we'll be close by to be reunited with her right away."

Kemp pulled at his bearded chin as he continued to frown in thought. "Well . . . I don't know. What do you think, Sergeant?"

Monroe leaned over and spat on the ground. "Speakin' frankly, sir, I don't like the idea. Havin' civilians around when you're goin' up against Injuns is never a good idea."

Jessie said, "It would mean the world to Whit and me not to have to wait to see Emily again. Besides, the three of us could take her home, and you and your men could continue with your patrol. You wouldn't have to worry about what to do with her."

Kemp nodded. "That's true."

"Lieutenant, I—"

Kemp forestalled Monroe's protest. "That's enough, Sergeant. I've made up my mind. Miss Franklin and her brother and Mr. Fargo will be allowed to accompany us. We might even be able to put Mr. Fargo's scouting abilities to work for us." He looked at Fargo. "What do you say?"

Fargo nodded. "I reckon I could lend a hand if you want me to."

"If you're as good a scout as your reputation, we can certainly use you."

Monroe scowled darkly, but he didn't argue with the lieutenant's decision. "The men have been restin' their horses while we talked. Are you ready to move out again, sir?"

"That's right. Pass the order. We'll be following the tracks of the hostiles to the northwest."

"Yes, sir."

"Would you care to join me at the head of the column, Mr. Fargo?"

"I will in a minute," Fargo said. "I want to talk to Whit and Jessie first. You'll be able to see the tracks."

"Very well." Kemp turned his horse and trotted back to his men, taking up position at the front of the patrol.

Fargo smiled tightly at Jessie. "Pretty smart move, getting him to agree to us coming along."

"Well, it was either that or pretend to turn back and then circle around and get ahead of them."

"I thought about that, too."

"But I thought we might as well take advantage of their presence, just in case we run into any trouble. You'll keep them from getting too close to the Indians and alerting them that we're back here, won't you?"

Fargo nodded. "That's what I had in mind."

"And then tonight, maybe, we can slip away and you can go after Emily just as you planned."

Fargo nodded again.

Whit had been looking back and forth between them as they talked. Now he said, "How did the two of you figure all that out without even talking to each other?"

"You know what they say, Whit." Jessie smiled at her brother. "Great minds work alike. Right, Skye?"

"I reckon we'll find out," Fargo said.

Lt. Kemp allowed Whit and Jessie to ride at the head of the column with him and Fargo. Fargo suggested that he ride on ahead alone and try to determine just how much of a lead the Comanches had on them. Kemp nodded in agreement.

Jessie brought her horse closer to Fargo's Ovaro. "You be careful, Skye," she said. "I don't want anything happening to you."

"Don't worry. I'll be back." Fargo lifted a hand in farewell as he nudged the stallion into a trot. He glanced back and saw Jessie watching him ride away.

He saw Sgt. Monroe watching Jessie, too, and he didn't like the look on the sergeant's face.

He didn't think Monroe would try anything with Lt. Kemp and the rest of the troop there, though. Jessie ought to be safe enough until he got back, at least from Monroe.

Fargo let the Ovaro stretch his legs. The stallion seemed to enjoy it. The cavalry patrol fell farther and farther behind until Fargo could no longer see them when he glanced back over his shoulder. He could see the dust raised by their horses, though. That was the main danger they faced in trailing the war party. If they got too close, the dust would give them away.

When he was a mile or more ahead of the troop, he slowed the Ovaro to an easy lope. He didn't want to catch up to the Comanches too quickly. That ran the risk of alerting them to his presence. As he stopped from time to time and studied the droppings left on the trail, though, he could tell that he was cutting steadily into the war party's lead. Now that they were back in familiar territory where they felt safe, they weren't in any hurry at all.

By late afternoon, the Indians were no more than an hour ahead of him. Their tracks led straight toward a large mesa that loomed in the distance. Fargo frowned as he studied it. If the Comanches were to camp up there, it could make his job of freeing Emily more difficult. Sometimes the tops of the mesas in this area were accessible, but usually by only one trail, so that a single guard could keep anyone from getting into camp.

Fargo reined in and took out his field glasses. Shading the lenses with one hand so that sunlight wouldn't reflect off them, he studied the mesa. It took him only a second to find the trail that wound up the side to the top. The Comanches were already on it. He saw their ponies climbing steadily, although he was too far away to make out any details about the riders. He'd hoped to spot Emily Franklin and make sure she was still alive, but the distance was too great. Despite that, he was convinced the Comanches hadn't killed her. They would have left her body on the trail if they had.

Jessie and Whit weren't going to be happy about this when he got back to the cavalry patrol. Trying to steal Emily away from the war party tonight would be too risky.

Fargo didn't care that much about the danger to himself. He had lived an adventurous existence, and although he savored life and everything it had to offer, he knew that he wasn't likely to die in bed.

But if the Indians caught him trying to sneak into their camp, they might figure he wasn't alone. They would torture him to death and possibly go ahead and kill Emily, too, just to simplify things for them. And they might double back and attack the patrol as well, putting Whit and Jessie in danger.

They would have to bide their time, that was all there was to it. Fargo turned and rode back the way he had come.

The sun was about to dip below the horizon by the time he spotted the patrol coming toward him. Fargo pulled the stallion back to a walk. As he approached, he saw Jessie spur out ahead of the others, ignoring Lt. Kemp's call for her to come back.

She brought her mount to a hurried stop in front of Fargo. "Did you find her? Did you see Emily?"

"I found the war party. They were climbing up to the top of a mesa to camp for the night. I didn't see Emily, no, but I'm sure she's still with them."

"How can you be so certain?"

"We haven't found her body," Fargo said.

Jessie gave a grim-faced nod. "That's true. And they wouldn't have bothered to hide it if they had killed her, would they?"

"No. They wouldn't have."

Whit and Lt. Kemp rode up then, followed by Sgt. Monroe and the rest of the troopers. Fargo quickly filled them in on what he had discovered.

"What do you suggest we do?" Kemp asked.

Monroe took exception to that. "This fella's just a scout, Lieutenant, and an unofficial one, at that. It's up to you to decide what we do."

"I know that, Sergeant. I'm merely asking for Mr. Fargo's advice."

"I think we'd better wait," Fargo said. "It's too risky trying to get to the top of that mesa and then back down with Miss Franklin. Maybe tomorrow night they'll make camp in some place that'll be easier for us to do what we need to do."

Kemp nodded. "That makes sense. We don't want to engage the hostiles until we have the best chance of defeating them."

"And the best chance of rescuing Miss Franklin."

"Yes, well, of course. That goes without saying."

Fargo wasn't convinced of that. He had a hunch Lt. Kemp would sacrifice Emily's life if it meant wiping out a Comanche war party and heaping some glory on himself.

It was up to him to make sure that didn't happen.

While on his way back to rejoin the cavalry patrol, Fargo had noticed a small draw about half a mile away. He told Kemp about it now and added, "That would be a good place to camp for the night. You can build a small fire in there without it being seen for miles around and have some hot food tonight. Otherwise you'll have to make a cold camp."

Kemp nodded. "That sounds like a good idea to me." He turned to Monroe. "Sergeant?"

"Whatever you want, sir." Monroe's reply was voiced in a surly enough tone to border on insubordination. "You're in command."

"Yes, I am." Kemp nodded to the Trailsman. "Lead the way, Mr. Fargo."

Within a half hour, Fargo had herded the patrol into the draw. They stopped not far from the mouth of it. It was possible to get caught in a flash flood in a place like this, even when there was no rain in the immediate vicinity. The sky was clear as far as the eye could see, though, except for a few high streaks of cloud that turned orange and gold and pink in the rays of the setting sun. Fargo thought they would be safe here, but they were close enough to the end of the draw that they could get out in a hurry if they needed to.

He found a good place next to the bank for a fire and pointed it out to the lieutenant. Kemp ordered a couple of his men to gather some wood. There were enough dead mesquite branches lying around to fuel a decent fire.

The rest of the troopers tended to the horses. Fargo unsaddled the Ovaro and Jessie's horse while Whit took care of his mount and the extra horse they had brought with them.

Jessie stood near Fargo while he was working with the horses and said, "Sergeant Monroe kept looking at me while you were gone, Skye. I don't like him."

"Neither do I. I've seen his type plenty of times before. He's used to running things in this troop. Probably up until now, Kemp has always asked his opinion about everything and then done whatever Monroe said, since Kemp doesn't have any experience."

"But then you came along, and the lieutenant is paying attention to your advice instead."

Fargo nodded. "Yeah. That's about the size of it."

"Be careful, Skye. I don't trust that man."

With a smile, Fargo said, "I'm sort of in the habit of being careful to start with. But I know what you mean."

Soon the smells of bacon and coffee filled the draw. The trooper in charge of the fire kept the flames low, so they wouldn't create a glow in the sky. Fargo offered to pitch in some supplies from the packs they had brought along, but Lt. Kemp refused.

"We brought along plenty of provisions. We can easily afford to share our food with the three of you."

"Better be careful, Lieutenant," Monroe said. "We don't know how long we'll have to stay out here chasin' those red heathens."

"That's true. But there's game out here, isn't there, Mr. Fargo?"

"Some," Fargo said. "Most of the big buffalo herds graze well north of here, especially at this time of year, but we might run across a few of the critters. There are deer and wild turkeys in these parts, too."

"So you see, Sergeant, we'll get by just fine, even if we have to forage part of the time."

"Yes, sir." The scowl that Monroe directed at Fargo said that was one more mark against the Trailsman as far as he was concerned.

By the time everyone was finished with supper, the fire had burned down to embers and full darkness had fallen. Kemp told Monroe to set up sentry details. The noncom picked out several of the troopers to take turns standing guard.

"I don't mind taking a turn, too," Fargo said.

Kemp shook his head. "That won't be necessary. We're perfectly capable of carrying out those duties, Mr. Fargo."

Fargo wasn't so sure of that. He'd been studying the troopers, and while a few of them seemed to be old, experienced hands like Sgt. Monroe, a lot of them struck him as being pretty green. He could tell by their accents that most of them were Easterners, probably youngsters who had joined the army because they didn't want to break their backs behind a plow on the family farm. This might even be the first patrol for some of them.

But he slept pretty lightly most of the time anyway, and the Ovaro was nearby and would alert him if he sensed any hostiles skulking around. Fargo nodded to Kemp and said, "If that's how you want it, Lieutenant. I'm going to take my bedroll up the draw a ways."

A chilly tone edged into Kemp's voice. "You don't care for our company, Mr. Fargo?"

"I just like to spread out a little at night. It's better not to be bunched up if trouble comes along."

"Trouble . . . in the form of that Comanche war party?"

Fargo shrugged. "I don't think they know we're back here, but I can't guarantee that."

"Very well. I'll see you in the morning."

Fargo had slung his bedroll over his shoulder and was about to move off up the draw when Jessie came up beside him, carrying her blankets.

"I'm going with you, Skye."

Fargo frowned. "I'm not sure that'd be proper."

"I don't give a damn about proper. If those savages attack us, I want to be with you. I think I'll have a better chance of surviving that way."

"Well, when you put it like that . . ." Fargo chuckled. "Don't blame me if your brother gets a mite upset about it, though."

"I'm not worried about what Whit thinks."

"Suit yourself."

The two of them walked about a hundred yards up the draw. Fargo noticed that Whit saw them going, but the young man didn't say anything. Maybe he had learned by now that he would be wasting his time by arguing with Jessie.

Fargo found a good, level spot for them to spread their blankets. "Go ahead and turn in," he told Jessie. "I'm going to take a look around first."

"Checking for trouble?"

"Something like that."

Fargo climbed to the top of the bank and hunkered there on his heels for several minutes, listening to the night. He sent all his senses out into the darkness, trusting to his instincts to tell him if any sort of danger threatened. He heard the rustle of some small animal moving around in the brush, the slither of a snake along the sandy ground, the faint flapping of wings as some night bird cruised overhead. He smelled dust and vegetation and earth. That was all.

Satisfied that he didn't need to worry—for the moment—he slid back down the bank to the spot where he had spread his blankets.

He wasn't surprised that Jessie was there waiting for him.

She sat on the blankets with her knees drawn up and her arms around them. The starlight struck highlights off her fair hair. She didn't look around as Fargo sat down beside her.

"Are you sure this is a good idea?" he asked.

"I told you, I'm a girl who gets what she goes after."

"Folks don't always get what they want."

She turned her head. In the night shadows, he couldn't see her eyes, but he heard the husky desire in her voice as she said, "This isn't what I want, Skye. It's what I need."

"In that case . . ."

Fargo leaned closer to her and brought his mouth down on hers.

Her arms went around his neck as she matched the hungry intensity of his kiss. Her lips parted to accept the invasion of his tongue as it probed into the warm, wet cavern of her mouth.

She surged closer to him, the warm mounds of her breasts pressing against his chest. Fargo brought up a hand between them and cupped one of those mounds. He felt her nipple hardening against his palm. He shifted his grip so that he could stroke the erect bud with his thumb. Jessie made a little moaning sound deep in her throat and tightened her embrace around his neck.

Still holding her and kissing her, Fargo laid her back on the blankets. He slid his hand up the split riding skirt she was wearing. Jessie gasped as he found her already slick core and delved a finger into it.

"You'd better kiss me again, Skye," she whispered. "Otherwise, I'm going to have a hard time keeping quiet . . ."

Fargo obliged, finding her mouth with his and relishing the hot, wet sweetness of it. He moved his finger inside her and made her hips thrust and sway with growing passion as he used his other hand to strip her of her clothes. He had to take his finger out of her to pull her skirt off, and she made a little sound of loss as he slid out.

She wasn't disappointed for long, though. Her hands tugged at his buckskins, urging him to get them off. Neither one of them was completely nude by the time Fargo moved between her widespread thighs, but they had bared enough flesh to accomplish their goal. His shaft was as hard as an iron bar by now, a long, thick pole jutting out proudly from his groin. Jessie wrapped both hands around it and moaned in her need to feel his manhood inside her. She brought it to her drenched opening, and Fargo sheathed himself fully within her with one strong thrust. Jessie threw her arms around his neck and hung on for dear life as he began to pump in and out of her. Her hips bucked eagerly as she met his thrusts with thrusts of her own.

Fargo sensed that neither of them wanted to delay their culmination. They were on a grim, dangerous mission in the middle of a hostile land, and at this moment, they needed the comfort they could take from each other. For several minutes, Fargo drove powerfully into her, taking both of them higher and higher toward the crest they sought, and then, when the moment was right, he penetrated her as deeply as he could and stayed buried in those depths as his climax seized him. Jessie shuddered underneath him in a climax of her own as Fargo emptied himself inside her in a series of throbbing spasms.

When it was over, they held each other as they glided down the far slope of their shared passion. Jessie snuggled into his shoulder.

"You don't know how much that meant to me, Skye. It gives me faith now that . . . that somehow, everything will work out all right." Suddenly, she pushed herself up on an elbow. "Oh, Lord! I didn't just jinx us, did I?"

Fargo laughed as he put his arms around her again and pulled her tighter against him. "We make our own luck, Jessie," he told her.

"Then I'll trust to the luck of the Trailsman."

And he wouldn't let her down, Fargo vowed to himself.

7

Fargo went to sleep with Jessie in his arms, but when he woke up sometime later in the night, she was gone. He felt a moment of alarm, as well as chagrin that she could have slipped away without him noticing, but then the worry eased as he heard someone moving around in the brush near the spot where they had spread their blankets. He figured that Jessie had just had some personal business she needed to attend to.

He sat up anyway and moved his hand closer to the butt of the Colt. He had coiled the shell belt and holster together and placed them close by when he took them off earlier. His Henry rifle lay there beside the blankets, too, where it would be handy if he should happen to need it.

The noises in the brush had gone silent. Fargo frowned. "Jessie!" he said in a low-pitched hiss. She should have been back by now.

A sudden crackle of branches and rattle of mesquite beans came to Fargo's ears. He drew the gun and stood up, wearing only his buckskin trousers.

"Jessie!" he said again.

This time he heard a muffled cry and the smack of a fist against flesh in response to his call. Biting back a curse, Fargo leaped toward the sounds, certain now that something was wrong.

The mesquites clawed at his bare skin as he ran into the thicket. His keen eyes caught sight of a pair of struggling figures. The larger one raised a fist and brought it down hard. The smaller figure slumped to the ground.

"Hold it!" Fargo said as he leveled his gun at the man who was still on his feet.

The man snarled something and lunged forward. If he had slapped leather, Fargo would have shot him, but as it was, Fargo hesitated for a split second. He wasn't going to gun down a man who wasn't trying to shoot him.

That gave the man time to plow into Fargo and knock him backward off his feet. They both went down, with the shadowy assailant landing on top of the Trailsman.

The impact jolted the revolver out of Fargo's hand. Fargo gasped for breath as the man drove a knee into his belly. From the crushing weight on top of him, Fargo guessed he was fighting Sgt. Monroe. Monroe was the only man in the troop as big as the hombre who now tried to slug a fist into the middle of Fargo's face.

Fargo sensed as much as saw the blow coming and jerked his head aside. Monroe howled in pain as he slammed his fist against the hard ground. Fargo reached up, grabbed the front of the sergeant's uniform blouse, and heaved him to the side. The move sent Monroe rolling away a few feet. Fargo rolled the other way and came up on his hands and knees. He dragged air into his lungs.

Monroe wasn't ready to give up the fight, not by a long shot. Fargo knew that. For some reason, Monroe had resented and disliked him on sight, and those sour feelings had been festering inside the noncom all day. This fight wouldn't be over until one—or both—of the two men could no longer rise and throw a punch. Fargo doubted that Monroe would stop even if Lt. Kemp ordered him to.

Because of that, Fargo couldn't allow himself to worry right now about whoever it was that Monroe had knocked down a moment earlier. He was sure it was Jessie the sergeant had been struggling with, and he wanted to make sure she was all right.

But if he turned his back on Monroe, the burly noncom would knock him out, too, and then Jessie would be left at the mercy of Monroe. Fargo didn't have any confidence that Kemp could control the man, and the other troopers wouldn't interfere with Monroe. Fargo had seen the way those green recruits looked at him in fear. Nor would Whit Franklin be a match for Monroe, any more than he had been for Aaron Sabin back in Weatherford.

So it was up to him to finish this fight, Fargo told himself. He spread his feet a little and braced himself as Monroe surged to his feet and charged at him with an enraged bellow. The sergeant swung malletlike fists in looping, powerhouse blows. If one of those punches connected, it might take Fargo's head off.

Fargo didn't intend to let any of them find their target.

He ducked under Monroe's sweeping punches and bored in on the sergeant, hammering his fists into Monroe's midsection. Monroe grunted and tried to grab Fargo in a bear hug, but the Trailsman darted back out of reach. The missed grab threw Monroe off balance. Fargo kicked his right leg out from under him.

Monroe toppled, but one long arm shot out as he fell. He managed to snag Fargo's leg and pulled him down with him. Monroe sank a knee into Fargo's belly. As Fargo gasped for breath, Monroe clubbed him in the head with a fist. For a second, the Trailsman saw stars.

That gave Monroe time to roll on top of him and take him by the throat. Even though his head was spinning from the blow Monroe had landed, Fargo knew he couldn't allow the sergeant to lock his grip. He cupped his hands and slapped them hard against Monroe's ears. Monroe threw his head back and howled in pain.

Fargo jabbed a stiff hand into Monroe's solar plexus, making the burly noncom gasp for air, too. Grabbing the front of Monroe's shirt, Fargo lifted himself and butted Monroe in the face. He shoved the stunned Monroe to the side and rolled the other direction. He made it to his feet just ahead of Monroe and had already launched a punch by the time Monroe surged off the ground. Fargo's fist smacked cleanly into Monroe's jaw with the sound of an ax biting deep into a chunk of firewood.

Even though Monroe was bigger, Fargo's punch packed

enough impact to knock the sergeant off his feet. Monroe sailed backward and crashed to the ground with bone-jarring force. He moaned, lifted his head and shook it for a second, then let it slump back to the ground underneath him. He didn't try to get up again.

As Fargo stood there, his broad, muscular chest heaving from the exertion of the fight, he became aware that the commotion had drawn the rest of the troop. They stood watching him, holding their rifles.

Lt. Kemp strode forward from the group and came to a stop in front of the Trailsman. "What's the meaning of this, Mr. Fargo? Why are you brawling with my sergeant?"

Fargo didn't have to answer that. Jessie stepped out of the brush, holding her torn shirt together so that it covered her.

"I can tell you what happened, Lieutenant. Sergeant Monroe tried to assault me. Skye stopped him."

Kemp's gaze switched back to Fargo. "Is that true?"

Fargo nodded. "It is. I heard him struggling with Miss Franklin and went to help her. Monroe didn't take kindly to it."

"Perhaps he thought Miss Franklin might welcome his attentions, seeing that she had gone up the draw with you earlier."

Whit had come up to see what was going on, too, and as he heard Kemp's sneering comment, he erupted in anger.

"Hey! I don't care if you *are* an officer—you can't talk about my sister like that!"

He moved closer to Kemp with his fists clenched, obviously ready to throw a punch. The tension grew as the troopers lifted their rifles and got ready to defend their commander.

Jessie got between Whit and Kemp and faced her brother angrily. "Back off, Whit," she told him. "I appreciate what you're trying to do, but this isn't the time or place."

His jaw thrust out. "Yeah, well, I'm gettin' used to having to defend you when folks start sayin' bad things about you. Maybe I wouldn't have to if you weren't such a—"

She slapped him before he could finish, her hand cracking

loudly across his face. Then as he stepped back in shock, she immediately clutched his arm and said, "Oh, God, I'm sorry, Whit. I didn't mean to do that. I just . . . I'm sorry, all right?"

While Whit looked at her, his face a mask, Fargo turned to Kemp. "Lieutenant, I think it'd be wise if you had a couple of your men help Sergeant Monroe back to his bedroll. And the men who were standing guard need to get back to their posts."

Kemp nodded, but his spine and his voice were still stiff. "You're right, of course."

He snapped the order to his men. It took three of the troopers to help Monroe to his feet and lead him off toward the camp. The sergeant cast a muddled but hate-filled glance toward Fargo as he went.

"I assure you, I'll be investigating this matter," Kemp continued to Fargo. "And I *will* get to the bottom of it. But right now, we have more pressing concerns. For that reason, I've changed my mind. In the morning, you three civilians will turn around and start back to where you came from."

"No!" Jessie said. "You can't do that, Lieutenant. You promised we could go with you so we can be there when you free Emily."

Kemp gave a stubborn shake of his head. "I never should have involved civilians in the first place. We'll carry out our mission, as ordered, and engage the hostiles at the first suitable opportunity."

"So you're just throwing away my sister's life!"

"Not at all. I'll do everything in my power to see to it that the other Miss Franklin survives . . . but not at the cost of our mission."

Fargo's mouth tightened into a grim line. "I don't reckon there's any chance of you changing your mind, Lieutenant?"

"None at all."

"I suppose that's it, then. We'll start back in the morning."

Jessie turned toward Fargo in surprise. "Skye! You can't mean that!"

"Lieutenant Kemp's in charge. We can't go against what

he says without going against the whole army, and I'm not prepared to do that."

"So you're giving up." Bitter resignation filled Whit's voice.

Jessie suddenly stepped up to Fargo and pounded a fist on his bare chest. "You bastard! And after I—" She choked off the rest of what she'd been about to say.

Kemp waved the rest of his troopers back to their blankets, except for the sentries, who resumed their posts. They were lucky no war parties had come along to jump them while all the ruckus was going on, Fargo thought.

"You may have to make yourself available for a hearing, Mr. Fargo," Kemp said. "Assaulting a member of the United States Army is nothing to take lightly. You'll remain in Weatherford until I get in touch with you following our return to Fort Griffin?"

"Are you ordering me to do that?"

"Yes, I am."

Fargo shrugged. "Then I reckon I'll be there."

Kemp gave him a curt nod and then stalked off after the others.

"That . . . that little stuffed shirt!" Jessie said. She turned sharply toward Fargo. "And you! You're not much better, you—"

"Let everybody get good and settled down again. Then the two of you can slip away along the draw. I'll get the horses and follow."

"You mean we're *not* going back to Weatherford like you said?" Whit sounded confused.

"Of course not," Jessie said as a smile appeared on her face. "It was all an act, wasn't it, Skye?"

Fargo chuckled. "Yeah, and you did a good job of sounding like you really believed I was a sorry son of a bitch."

"Yes, well, I . . . uh . . ."

"Don't worry about it," Fargo told her. "The important thing is that before the night's over, we'll be on our way after your sister again. And we won't turn back until she's with us, safe and sound."

Fargo hoped that was a promise he could keep.

* * *

Whit gathered up his gear and moved up the draw to spread his blankets close to Fargo and Jessie. None of the troopers would think that was anything unusual, given what had happened earlier. The three of them settled down and pretended to be asleep. When plenty of snoring had started to come from the camp, Fargo whispered instructions to his two companions.

Jessie and Whit got up and gathered their things as quietly as possible, then stole up the draw away from the cavalry camp. Fargo waited until he was sure they were well clear without any of the sentries noticing that they were gone. Then he moved with catlike grace and silence toward the horses, staying in the shadows as much as possible.

The horses had been left saddled at Fargo's suggestion, although the cinches had been loosened. In the middle of Comanche country, where they might have to run for their lives at a second's notice, taking the time to saddle the horses might have proved fatal. One by one, Fargo went to the mounts he and Jessie and Whit had been using and tightened the cinches. He did the same on the extra horse they had brought for Emily. Then he gathered up their reins, and those of the packhorse, and led the animals away from the troopers' horses. He listened intently as he did so for any sounds of alarm.

The troopers who were sleeping kept snoring, undisturbed by the soft hoofbeats of the horses. Fargo knew he couldn't count on all the guards being careless, though, and sure enough, he hadn't gone twenty yards when one of the sentries called quietly in an Eastern-accented voice, "Hey! Who's that? What are you doing?"

Fargo stuck his foot in the stirrup and vaulted onto the Ovaro's back. He dug the heels of his boots into the stallion's flanks and sent the big black-and-white horse leaping forward. He hung on tightly to the reins of the other horses. They galloped after the Ovaro.

"Halt! Halt!" The shouts came from the guard who had heard Fargo leaving with the horses. "Stop or I'll shoot! Hey! Lieutenant! Help! Somebody's stealin' the horses!"

Fargo heard Kemp's startled response over the hoofbeats that echoed back from the wall of the draw. "Stop them! Shoot them if you have to!"

Fargo had reconnoitered enough earlier to know that the draw made a sharp bend about two hundred yards from the camp. He had told Jessie and Whit to wait right around that bend. He would pick them up there. As soon as he reached it, he would be out of the line of fire.

Of course, he had to get there first. He figured the troopers wouldn't be very good shots in this dim light. In fact, he was sort of counting on that hope to keep him alive.

Carbines blasted behind him. He leaned forward over the Ovaro's neck to make himself a smaller target. A single bullet whined past his head close enough for him to hear it, but as far as he could tell, that was the best shot of the hurried fusillade. Neither the stallion nor any of the other horses broke stride as they raced along the draw toward the bend.

Fargo slowed slightly to make the turn and haul the other horses around it with him. As he brought them to a stop, Jessie and Whit hurried over from where they had been crouched against the bank and threw their bedrolls and saddlebags over their horses. A moment later, they were mounted.

"Let's go!" Fargo said.

He still had the reins of the extra horse and the pack animal. That was the way he wanted it, because while Jessie and Whit both seemed to be good riders, they had all they could handle just staying in the saddle during this breakneck dash through the darkness. Even though Fargo knew it would take several minutes for the cavalry patrol to get organized, mount up, and come after them, there was no time to waste.

Assuming, of course, that Lt. Kemp decided to give chase. There was no real reason for him to do so. They hadn't taken anything except what belonged to them. Fargo expected that Kemp's stiff-necked pride would demand that he come after them, though.

Fargo planned to give the pursuit the slip before Kemp and the troopers had a chance to catch up. He kept his eyes open for a way out of the draw, and when he came to a place where the bank had caved in, he waved a hand toward it.

"Over there! Follow me!"

The Ovaro took the rough slope without hesitation, picking his way up it with the deftness of a mountain goat. The other horses found it slower going, so Fargo had to hold the stallion back a little. When they reached the top, he reined in and turned in the saddle to wait for Jessie and Whit.

Now that he was stopped, he could hear hoofbeats back down the draw. The troopers were coming after them, all right. Fargo figured Kemp was livid at this blatant defiance of his orders.

The horses carrying Jessie and Whit struggled to the top of the caved-in bank. Fargo gave them a few seconds to rest, then said, "Come on. Stay as close to me as you can."

They were out on the flats now. The mesa where the Comanche war party had camped loomed in the distance, visible even in the starlight as a dark bulk. Fargo spotted a wink of orange light atop it. The Indians had built a fire for their camp. No reason for them not to. They felt safe here in their usual stomping grounds.

If Fargo had been by himself, he would have been confident that he could outrun the cavalry on the Ovaro. He wasn't so sure about his companions, though. He continued holding the stallion in so that he wouldn't race too far ahead of them.

Half an hour later, they came to a small ridge. Fargo led Jessie and Whit behind it. They were far enough ahead of the troopers that he didn't think Kemp would be able to follow for much longer. He waved the other two on ahead of him and paused to listen again for sounds of pursuit.

A tight grin appeared on Fargo's bearded face as he heard hoofbeats in the distance. They were receding instead of coming closer. Kemp must have gotten turned around in the dark and headed off in the wrong direction. With a grim chuckle, Fargo started after Jessie and Whit.

When he caught up to them, he said, "Kemp's not going to catch us now. He's gone the wrong way."

"What are we going to do?" Jessie asked.

"Find a place to hole up for the night. Then tomorrow we'll get back on the trail of that war party and wait for our chance to take Emily away from them."

"We won't have the cavalry to keep them from chasing us now."

Fargo shook his head. "That's right—we won't. But we won't have to worry about Kemp starting a fight with those Comanches just so he can try to win a medal or two. That was a surefire way to get Emily killed."

Whit asked, "How do we know the lieutenant and the rest of the soldiers won't catch up to the Comanches before we do and ruin everything anyway?"

"Not likely. I reckon even Kemp can follow those tracks, but we can move faster, and after tonight, we'll be ahead of him to start with. He's liable to wander around out here most of the night looking for us, and that'll wear out his horses. He'll have to take it slow tomorrow or risk riding them into the ground. He won't want to be set afoot out here in the middle of Comancheria."

They seemed to accept that explanation. A short time later, Fargo found a little cave in the side of a bluff. They led the horses inside, where Fargo risked lighting a match. He cupped the flame in his hand so that it couldn't be seen from outside, but the faint glow was enough to let them see that the cave was empty of rattlesnakes or other varmints. They loosened the cinches on the saddles again. Then Fargo said, "We'll need to take turns standing guard. Whit, you take the first watch. Can you stay awake?"

Whit nodded. "Yeah, I think so."

"You'd better be sure. We don't want anybody sneaking up on us, white or red."

"I'll be fine."

"All right. I'll take the second watch, and you can finish up, Jessie." That arrangement would put the responsibility for keeping up with the guard changes on Fargo. That was best, he decided, because he had the true frontiersman's instinct for telling time by the stars.

He and Jessie rolled up in their blankets. Fargo fell asleep right away and rested soundly for several hours, then woke up at the proper time.

"Hear anything unusual?" he asked Whit in a whisper, so as not to disturb Jessie's slumber.

Whit shook his head. "I didn't hear much of anything. Some coyotes howling off in the distance, but that's all. *If* they were really coyotes. I remember back at the ranch—"

"I'd bet a hat the ones you heard tonight were the real thing," Fargo said. "Out here the Comanches don't need to be signaling each other like that."

"Yeah." Whit stifled a yawn. "Reckon I'll turn in. It's been a long night. Hell, it's been a long *week.*"

Fargo couldn't argue with that.

For the next few hours, he sat in the mouth of the cave with his knees up and the Henry rifle beside him. Whit had been right. The night was about as quiet and peaceful as could be. He couldn't hear the cavalry patrol blundering around anymore, and he wondered if Kemp had given up and gone back to the camp in the draw. He hoped they had seen the last of Kemp, Monroe, and the rest of the troopers, at least until they had gotten Emily back from the Indians.

When it came time to wake Jessie for the last couple of hours of standing watch, Fargo moved over beside her and put a hand on her shoulder. She gasped a little as she came awake. Fargo said, "It's all right," and she heaved a sigh of relief.

"Skye," she whispered. "I was having a terrible dream, all about the Indians and that horrible Sergeant Monroe . . ."

"What happened back there, anyway? How did he manage to grab you?"

Jessie sat up and yawned. "I had to go off in the bushes to—well, you know. Monroe must have been watching and waiting for his chance. He came up behind me and clapped a hand over my mouth. He said . . . well, he said some vile things about how since you'd had me, he was going to, as well." Her voice dropped to an even softer level. "Whit's right. I'm a shameless hussy."

"The hell you are. You're just a woman who knows what you want. If more people were like that, men and women both, the world would be a simpler place."

"Maybe you're right." She leaned her head against his shoulder for a moment, then straightened. "Now, you go and get some more sleep. I'll stay awake and watch. I promise."

Fargo stretched out and wrapped up in his blanket. Despite the heat of the days in Texas at this time of year, the air cooled off quickly at night and held a slight chill by these predawn hours. He dropped off to sleep instantly.

Fargo was up again before dawn. They had a cold, skimpy breakfast of leftover biscuits and salt pork and were in their saddles again by the time the sky had begun to turn pink and gold in the east. Fargo led the way, keeping his eyes open for the cavalry patrol. Even though he was convinced that Lt. Kemp had no idea where they were, it was always possible that the troopers could stumble onto them by accident.

They circled wide to the west around the mesa where the war party had camped the night before. Fargo suspected the Indians were already gone this morning, but he couldn't be sure of that. The tracks would tell him the story.

The sun was up by the time he located the trail again. It still led northwestward. Jessie and Whit were exhausted despite the rest they had gotten. Fargo could tell that. But neither of them asked for any favors, and they grew enthusiastic again when Fargo pointed out the tracks the war party had left.

"Maybe today is the day we'll get Emily back," Jessie said.

Fargo hoped that turned out to be the case. He followed the trail, moving fast enough to keep up with the Indians without crowding them from behind.

By afternoon, the Comanches were still a mile or a mile and a half ahead. Fargo had a new worry, though. He spotted some riders moving along a ridge to the west. They had to be mighty confident in their safety to let themselves be skylighted like that, which meant they probably belonged to another band of Indians.

And the path they were on was going to cut right in between Fargo and his companions and the Comanches who had stolen Emily from Lost Valley.

8

Fargo pointed out the other riders to Jessie and Whit. With a worried expression on her face, Jessie asked, "Who do you think they are?"

"Hard to say. Could be another bunch of Comanches. Might be Lieutenant Kemp and those troopers, although I don't see how they could have gotten over there that fast." Fargo shook his head. "I can't think of anybody else it could be. I reckon we'd better steer clear of whoever it is, though. I don't see how they could be friendly to us."

"They're fixin' to get between us and the Indians," Whit pointed out.

Fargo nodded. "We'll find a place to wait. Maybe they'll go on past."

"That'll put us that much farther behind Emily." Whit sighed. "I reckon you're right, though. Best not to take a chance."

They were already taking enough chances just by being out here in the middle of this hostile landscape, Fargo thought.

A few minutes later, they came to a knob topped by a cluster of scrubby mesquite trees. Fargo motioned for his companions to stop and dismount. After he had swung down from the saddle, he handed the reins of the extra horse and the pack animal to Whit and then pulled his Henry from its sheath.

"I'm going up to the top of this little hill to keep an eye on those strangers." Fargo took the field glasses from his saddlebags as well. "Wait here."

"I'll come with you," Jessie said.

"Suit yourself."

Whit didn't look too happy about that, but he didn't say anything.

Fargo and Jessie climbed to the top of the knob and stretched out on their bellies under the mesquites. Fargo propped himself on his elbows and brought the field glasses to his eyes. The powerful lenses seemed to bring the riders a lot closer when he peered through them.

He stiffened in surprise when he saw that the strangers were white men, but not the cavalry patrol. Instead of blue uniforms, they wore a variety of rough clothing and broad-brimmed hats. Most of them were bearded. They were well armed, too, with rifles, shotguns, and revolvers. Several of the men carried Sharps Big Fifties across their saddles. Fargo was even more surprised when he turned the glasses toward the rear of the party and saw a wagon trundling along behind the riders, being drawn by a team of big, rawboned mules.

"Son of a gun," Fargo breathed.

"What is it, Skye? Who are they?"

Fargo lowered the field glasses. "Looks like a group of hide hunters."

"Hide hunters?"

"Yeah. They go out after buffalo, kill them and skin them, and then sell the hides. Nobody ever thought of doing that until a few years ago. Nobody but the Indians, that is, and they just use the hides themselves instead of selling them. I've heard there's a trader who comes to Fort Griffin every now and then to buy buffalo hides."

"I don't know why anybody would want one."

Fargo chuckled. "You won't find anything warmer than a buffalo robe. I've spent many a cold night wrapped up in one."

"With a squaw for company, no doubt."

Fargo didn't reply to that. He just lifted the glasses to his eyes again and studied the men in the distance some more.

After a moment, Jessie went on, "Maybe they'd be willing to help us get Emily back."

"I don't know. . . . Their ability to get in and out of here sort of depends on not letting the Comanches know that they're here. I'm not sure they'd want to announce their presence."

"Even to save Emily's life?"

"I suppose we could ask them."

"Hadn't we better get moving, then, before they go on past?"

Fargo nodded and started to scoot back away from the top of the hill. "Yeah, come on."

Whit was waiting for them with an anxious expression on his face. "Who are they?" he asked. "Are they going to cause trouble for us?"

"We can hope not." Fargo explained about the hide hunters. "We're going to intercept them now."

"Fine by me. Those Comanches will think twice about chasin' us if we've got a bunch of good shots on our side."

The three of them mounted up and rode out from behind the knob. Fargo set a fast pace, still following the trail of the Comanches. He knew the other riders must have seen them coming, because he could tell from the dust they'd been raising that the men had stopped, smack-dab on the path that Fargo and his companions were following.

Fargo had done a quick head count through the field glasses. There were a dozen of the strangers. The Comanches would outnumber them if it came to a fight, but if the men really were hide hunters, each of them would probably be worth two or three of the green cavalry troopers. They had to be hard-bitten hombres to risk their lives by penetrating into this region controlled by the hostiles, and good shots, too.

Fargo lifted a hand in greeting as he and Jessie and Whit rode up. He was close enough now to see suspicion in the eyes of the men, which came as no surprise. Out here in Comancheria, they would be on the lookout for trouble all the time, and they didn't know who Fargo and the others were.

One of the men spurred out to meet them. He wore a flat-crowned black hat and a vest made of buffalo hide. Several days' worth of dark stubble covered his lean, angular jaw. He gave Fargo a tight smile and a nod. Fargo couldn't help but notice that the man's left eye was milky and pointed off at an odd angle.

"Howdy," the man said. "Didn't expect to run across any other white folks out here." He reached up and tugged on the brim of his hat as he nodded to Jessie. "'Specially a lady. My name's McCall, ma'am. Luther McCall."

"I'm pleased to meet you, Mr. McCall," Jessie said, although Fargo could tell that she was nervous. "I'm Jessie Franklin. This is my brother, Whit, and Mr. Skye Fargo."

McCall's good eye shifted back to the Trailsman. "Skye Fargo, eh? I think I've heard of you."

Fargo didn't respond to that. Instead, he said, "We're on the trail of a white girl who was taken captive by the Comanches, down in the Brazos country."

McCall waved a hand at their surroundings. "Shoot, this is all Brazos country. The Double Mountain fork ain't more'n twenty miles north of here."

"I know," Fargo said with a nod. He gestured toward the ground. "You can see for yourself the tracks of the war party we're following."

McCall rasped a hand over his jaw. "Yeah, we done noticed the prints those unshod ponies left. Looks like a good-sized bunch. Been off on a raid, have they?"

"That's right." Fargo felt a twinge of impatience, but he knew not to rush McCall. A lot of frontiersmen liked to take their time and draw out any conversation, especially one with a stranger. So many of these men rode lonely trails much of the time. They hungered for company.

They hungered for female companionship, too, Fargo reminded himself. He had seen the way McCall's good eye looked over Jessie. The man hadn't been insulting about it, but he had noted appreciatively the curves of her body and the beauty of her face.

"The girl they took is called Emily Franklin," Fargo went on. "She's the sister of Jessie and Whit here."

McCall looked at Jessie again. "Beggin' your pardon, ma'am, but you hadn't ought to be out here. It ain't exactly safe in these parts for a bunch o' well-armed men, let alone a lady."

"I can ride and shoot, Mr. McCall. I came along to help get my sister back from those savages."

McCall chuckled. "Well, I do like your attitude, ma'am. You need a hand with the chore?"

"We were hoping you'd be willing to help out."

"Shoot, yeah. Can't leave no white girl in the hands o' them red heathens if we can do somethin' about it." McCall looked at Fargo again. "If you're the hombre I think you are, I reckon you got a plan."

Fargo nodded. "If we jump the Comanches, they'll just kill Emily first thing," he said, explaining the situation as he had to Lt. Kemp. McCall obviously grasped it much better than the lieutenant had, though. He nodded in agreement with what Fargo was saying. "I plan to sneak into their camp and get Emily away from them, then make a run for it."

"And you could use a hand fightin' off the Comanch' when they go to chasin' you."

"That's right, if you're willing."

"Well . . . that ain't why we come out here, but like I said . . . I reckon we ought to lend you a hand. I'll have to ask the other fellas how they feel about it, though. I won't ask any man to risk his life if he ain't willin'."

"I understand."

McCall turned his horse. "Be back in a minute."

He rode over to the other men and talked with them in low tones. Once he turned in his saddle and waved toward Fargo, Jessie, and Whit. Several of the men nodded enthusiastically. Fargo guessed they liked the idea of being able to help out a pretty girl.

Of course, he and his companions ran a risk by joining forces with the hide hunters. The men were a hard-looking bunch. They might decide to kill him and Whit and keep Jessie for themselves.

Fargo thought that was unlikely, though. Most frontiersmen, even the roughest hardcases, wouldn't molest a decent woman. Even whores were usually treated with a measure of respect. Sgt. Monroe's attack on Jessie was unusual in that way.

Luther McCall rode back to join them. "The rest of the bunch agrees with me, folks. We'll do what we can to help you get the gal back."

"Thank you, Mr. McCall," Jessie said. "We'll have a better chance with you along."

McCall grinned. "I reckon you will. Do we keep followin' those redskins, Fargo?"

"That's right. And I hope they make camp tonight in some place where I can get to Emily without too much trouble. Last night, they camped on a mesa south of here."

McCall nodded. "I know the place. This ain't our first time out here. And I can make a pretty good guess where they'll be stoppin' tonight."

Fargo leaned forward in the saddle. "Where?"

"There's a place called Buffalo Springs that's right on this war trail they're usin'. That's why we normally steer clear of it. But we know where it is. Good water, some graze for their ponies . . . That's where the varmints usually stop when there's a bunch of 'em travelin' through these parts."

Now that McCall mentioned it, Fargo recalled hearing of Buffalo Springs in the past. Even with his long years of adventuring and wandering, there were places on the frontier where he had never been, and that was one of them. He had heard old-timers speak of it, though.

"Instead of following them straight to it, maybe we should circle around and come at it from another direction," he suggested. "They'd be less likely to be watching that way."

McCall laughed and then spat. "I guarantee you, them savages ain't worried about anybody followin' 'em. They figure a white man'd be crazy to trail 'em this far into their territory." He laughed again. "And I ain't sure but what they're right!"

He turned his horse and waved for Fargo and the other two to follow him. Fargo felt a little odd about letting someone else lead the way. He was used to being the one in that position.

But McCall evidently knew this part of the country better than he did, so Fargo let him take the lead. The only important thing here was rescuing Emily Franklin from the Comanches. Fargo had never been the sort of man to let his own pride stand in the way of getting a job done. That just wasn't the way he was made.

He hoped McCall was right about the Indians stopping for the night at Buffalo Springs, though. Otherwise, it would cost them a lot of time to backtrack here and pick up the Comanches' trail again.

Jessie moved her horse a little closer to Fargo's Ovaro as they rode past the rest of the hide hunters. He knew she felt their eyes on her, and the scrutiny made her a little uneasy. The men kept any comments to themselves, though. They turned their horses and the mule-drawn wagon around and followed McCall and Fargo.

"How many trips have you made out here?" Fargo asked the leader of the hide hunters as the group circled back to the west, away from the Comanche war trail.

"I don't recollect exactly. Enough so that I know my way around and know how to avoid the Injuns." McCall shook his head. "Reckon this'll be the first time I've gone lookin' for 'em."

"How far is it to Buffalo Springs?"

McCall rubbed his jaw and frowned in thought. "About fifteen miles, I'd make it. Of course, the way we're circlin' around, we'll have more ground to cover than that. We should get there along about dark."

"We wouldn't want to get there any earlier, if that's where the Comanches are going to camp."

"Yeah, we don't want those redskins spottin' us."

"We appreciate you helping us. I hope it won't cause trouble for you in the future."

"Make the Comanch' more aware that we been comin' out here, you mean?" McCall shook his head. "I reckon some of 'em must know it already. They're bound to have seen our hoofprints and wagon tracks."

Fargo knew he was right about that. Probably not much went on in these parts that the Indians didn't know about.

The long, roundabout ride to Buffalo Springs took most of the day. The hide hunters shared their supplies for the midday meal, although the food wasn't any fancier than what Fargo and his companions had been having. And their coffee, which they brewed over a small, almost smokeless fire fueled by buffalo dung, wasn't as good as what Fargo usually made. Or maybe he was just used to his own coffee, having spent so much time alone in his life.

As they were riding that afternoon, Fargo tried to sound out Luther McCall about the hide-hunting business, but the man didn't seem to want to talk about it. "It's a bloody, smelly, nasty business," McCall said as his left eye wandered aimlessly. "Sort o' like life itself."

"You don't enjoy life?"

"It ain't a matter of enjoyin' . . . It's a matter of survivin'."

Fargo understood that attitude. Plenty of men on the frontier felt that way. They had to, because life out here could indeed be cruel and merciless at times. Not always, though, and Fargo never tried to lose sight of that. There was plenty about life to savor, too.

Late that afternoon, they came in sight of a patch of green in the distance. As they rode out in front of the others, McCall pointed it out to Fargo, who had already noticed the vegetation.

"That's the springs. If the Injuns ain't there already, I'm bettin' they will be soon."

"We'll wait until dark and make sure of it," Fargo said. "If they're camped there, I'll slip in and get Emily, then head back here as quick as we can without alerting the Comanches. If we're lucky, we might be able to get away without them even knowing that she's gone until morning."

McCall grinned. "That'd be a neat trick, wouldn't it? That's about what I'd expect, though, from the Trailsman. I've heard a heap of stories about you, Fargo."

"I can't promise that all of them are true."

"Hell, if even half of 'em are, you've led a mighty excitin' life. I've heard that you're quite a hand with the ladies, too." McCall glanced back over his shoulder at Jessie, who was riding with Whit about forty feet behind them. "That Miss Jessie is a mighty fine-lookin' gal."

"I can't argue with that."

"I hope we can get her sister back. I want to see that face o' hers light up in a smile."

That would be worth seeing, all right, Fargo thought.

They halted when they were still more than a mile from Buffalo Springs. When everyone had dismounted and the hide hunters were tending to their horses, McCall hunkered on his heels and started drawing in the dirt with a stick.

"This here's what it looks like up yonder. There's a little bluff, and that's where the springs come right out o' the rock face. They feed a pool that's formed there, with trees and grass around it. There's a place right here where another rock crops up from under the ground, and that's where the Injuns always build their campfire. They'll spread out around the pool to sleep, more'n likely. No tellin' where they'll put the prisoner."

"That's why I need to get up there and take a good look as soon as it starts to get dark," Fargo said. He knew that right after dusk was one of the hardest times for a sentry to see anything.

McCall nodded. "Yeah, that's the way to do it. I'll come with you."

Fargo hesitated. "I'm not sure that's a good idea. Be less chance of them spotting me if I'm alone."

"Don't worry. I've snuck up on Injuns before. I won't give us away. And if there is any trouble, two of us stand a better chance o' gettin' out than one man alone."

"All right. We'll wait a while, then start over there on foot."

Fargo went over to talk to Jessie and Whit. He explained the plan to them, then said, "Keep your eyes open while I'm gone. I don't expect any trouble from these men, but you can't ever be sure."

"All right, Skye," Jessie said. "You're not going to try to bring Emily back this time, are you?"

"No, this is just to scout out the place and make sure where they're keeping her. I'll go back later by myself to get her."

Whit said, "You better watch out for that fella McCall. Ma would say that fella's got an evil eye."

Fargo shook his head. "Just a wandering one."

"Be careful," Jessie urged him. "Now that we're this close to Emily, we don't want anything to go wrong."

"If I have anything to say about it, she'll be with you again before the night's over."

Of course, even if he kept that promise, they might be running for their lives from the Comanches at the time, he thought with a wry smile to himself.

The place where they had stopped wasn't a suitable campsite. There was no water and little cover. But they weren't planning to spend the night here. This was just a place for the others to wait while Fargo and McCall scouted the Indian camp, and then while Fargo made his daring foray into that camp to rescue Emily Franklin. The hide hunters passed the short time until dusk by tending to their horses and gnawing on some jerky from a box of supplies in the back of the wagon.

Some of them handed around a bottle of whiskey, too, which made Fargo frown. He liked a good drink as much as any man, but with them possibly facing a fight for their lives tonight, he didn't want anybody getting all muddled on liquor.

When he said something about it to McCall, though, the man just grinned and shook his head. "Don't worry about it, Fargo. I know those ol' boys. Some of 'em are better shots drunk than they are sober."

Fargo didn't believe that, but he didn't argue the matter. The hide hunters were volunteering their help, after all.

As shadows began to settle down over the landscape, Fargo saw the orange flicker of a fire through the trees at the springs. The Comanches were there, all right. Only the warriors who ruled this region would be bold enough to build such a big fire.

Fargo gave Jessie a hug and shook hands with Whit. "I'll be back in a while," he told them. "Then we'll wait until it's good and dark before I go and get Emily."

"Ready, Fargo?" McCall asked. He wasn't carrying his rifle, and Fargo had left the Henry in the saddle boot on the Ovaro, too. Neither man wanted to lug along a heavy weapon on this mission, the success of which depended mostly on stealth.

Fargo nodded. "Let's go."

The two men trotted off into the gloom.

It took them about a quarter of an hour to reach the springs. When they were still about three hundred yards away, they dropped to all fours and crawled closer, finally bellying down so that the Indians couldn't see them in the glow that extended outward from the campfire. They stopped at the edge of the light and studied what they could see from where they were.

The fire did a good job of lighting up the area around the springs. Fargo could see the rocks where the water trickled out to form the pool, and he saw as well the shapes moving around the fire. He heard laughter as the Comanche warriors talked among themselves. They seemed to be having a good time, with no worries in the world.

That wasn't the case for the figure who sat huddled at the edge of the pool, not far from the fire. Emily Franklin had her knees drawn up and her arms wrapped around them. Her shoulders were hunched over and her head was tipped forward. It looked to Fargo as if she were trying to make herself as small as possible, curling up in a ball to shut out the rest of the world. That might be her way of escaping the horrors she had been forced to endure.

As Fargo watched, one of Emily's captors walked over to the girl and spoke to her. She didn't look up or reply, and for a second, Fargo thought the Comanche was going to strike her. The Indian just gave a disgusted shake of his head, though, and walked away.

A few minutes later, two more of the Comanches approached Emily. Fargo's jaw tightened. He knew he might have to lie there and watch Emily being assaulted. Not doing anything to try to stop the attack would be difficult, but he knew he would have to control his anger. Chances were, Emily had already been raped numerous times during her captivity. Callous though it might seem, Fargo was more concerned right now with saving her life.

The two warriors just hunkered in front of her and talked to her, though. She finally looked up and shook her head in answer to something that one of them asked her. The Comanche stood up, went to the fire, and came back with a piece of meat he had ripped off the roasting carcass of some sort of animal. He offered the food to Emily and seemed to be insisting that she eat. Finally, with obvious reluctance, Emily took the haunch and started gnawing on it. The Indian who had given it to her nodded, stood up, and moved away from her, along with his companion.

"Looks like they ain't treatin' her too bad," Luther McCall whispered. "Right now, anyway."

"Yeah," Fargo said. Of course, it wasn't too surprising that Emily's captors were trying to get her to eat. They would want to keep her alive, as long as it wasn't too much trouble, so that they could take her back to the rest of their band and make a slave out of her. Eventually, one of the warriors might even marry her.

Fargo and McCall watched as Emily ate the meat. When she was finished, she even licked the grease off her fingers. Her hunger had gotten the better of the revulsion she must have felt at eating half-raw rabbit or prairie dog, whatever the varmint had been.

She stood up and motioned to the Indians. They ignored her at first, but her urgent gestures caught the attention of one of them after a moment. He stood up and came toward her. He laughed and made a crude motion indicating that she should squat and take care of her business right where she was. Emily gave a vehement shake of her head. The Comanche took hold of her arm and jerked her away from the pool, toward the edge of the circle of light cast by the campfire.

"Son of a bitch," McCall breathed. "Are you thinkin' what I'm thinkin', Fargo?"

"If we can jump that warrior and take Emily away from him without the others knowing, it'll be a while before they figure out that she's gone."

"Damn right. Luck's with us."

That was the way it looked. They had been presented with an opportunity to get Emily away from the Comanches here and now, and they'd be fools not to take it.

"Come on," Fargo whispered.

He crawled backward until he was well out of the light, then got to his feet and cat-footed around the springs, circling toward the spot where the Comanche had taken Emily to tend to her personal business. Fargo had no doubt that the Indian intended to stand there and watch her. He hoped that was the case.

That way, the Comanche would be less likely to notice Fargo coming up behind him.

Fargo heard Luther McCall following him. The hide hunter moved quietly, but not quite as stealthily as the Trailsman.

Ahead of them in the darkness, the Indian was talking. Fargo understood the Comanche tongue, although he wasn't exactly fluent in it. The warrior was making crude comments to Emily, trying to embarrass her. He laughed.

He wouldn't be laughing much longer, Fargo thought as he reached down to slide the Arkansas toothpick from its sheath on his leg. Silence was crucial. Fargo intended to come up behind the Comanche, clap one hand over his mouth, and use the other to drive the blade into the man's back and pierce his heart. If the thrust went home cleanly, the Comanche would die in a matter of seconds without making a sound.

Fargo's keen eyes picked out the warrior's shape as the

Comanche stood there with his back turned and his arms folded across his chest. Beyond him was another shape that belonged to Emily. Fargo was poised to strike, silent and lethal as a copperhead.

Something crashed into the back of his head with stunning force. The blow drove him forward. He staggered, trying to keep his balance and turn at the same time. McCall had betrayed him. That was the only answer.

His muscles refused to obey him. His legs folded up underneath him. He crashed to the ground as a darkness blacker than any night closed in on his brain. The last things Fargo was aware of were sounds in the distance. A sudden surprised shout, gunfire . . .

And a woman's scream.

9

Fargo was a little surprised that he was still alive. He knew he was, though, because his head hurt like hell, and that wouldn't be happening if he were dead.

He lay there with his eyes closed as his senses returned to him. A variety of sounds and smells filtered into his awareness.

He heard talk and laughter, and his brain was working well enough for him to recognize both English and Comanche words, although he couldn't yet put them together into understandable sentences. Someone not far away moaned in pain, too.

He smelled smoke from the campfire, roasting meat, unwashed flesh, tobacco, and whiskey.

His face was pressed into the dirt, because he was lying on his belly. There was grit in his mouth that made him want to spit, but he suppressed the impulse because he didn't want any of the men around him to know that he had regained consciousness.

His certainty that Luther McCall was the one who had struck him down from behind, plus the mingling of English and Comanche he heard, led him to one inescapable conclusion.

The men he had taken for hide hunters were really Comancheros.

Some people claimed that the Comancheros didn't really exist, that they were just a myth. But Fargo knew better. Some sixty or seventy years earlier, when New Mexico Territory had still been ruled by the Spanish, traders had risked their lives to travel into the northern part of the territory and across the border into what was now the Texas Panhandle in order to barter with the Comanches. They traded liquor, gunpowder, and guns for captives who were then taken down to Mexico and sold as slaves. Over the years, the unsavory practice had grown, but then it had faded somewhat due to the political upheavals in Mexico. Recently, however, Fargo had heard rumors that the Comancheros were becoming active in Texas again. This time they consisted mostly of white men, American outlaws rather than Mexican bandidos. Even though the hammering pain in Fargo's head made it difficult to think, his brain was starting to work again, and it told him that McCall and the other men had to be Comancheros.

McCall had played him for a fool, and that knowledge caused anger to burn fiercely inside the Trailsman. He vowed that he would settle the score with the man.

But first he had to stay alive.

Keeping his breathing slow and regular as if he were still unconscious, Fargo opened his eyes in narrow slits. He didn't move his head. He had only a tiny field of vision. He saw an orange glow to one side that probably came from a campfire, so he supposed that he'd been hauled in to the Comanche camp at Buffalo Springs.

He wasn't the only one. He saw Whit Franklin lying on the ground a few feet away. Whit's face was bloody from a gash on his forehead. Judging by the bruise surrounding the gash, the young man had been pistol-whipped and knocked unconscious. He was still out, although he shifted and moaned softly from time to time.

If he and Whit were prisoners, thought Fargo, then in all likelihood Jessie was, too. But he couldn't see her, and he wished he knew where she was and whether she was all right.

Suddenly, he heard Luther McCall's voice nearby, and by now the clamor inside his skull had subsided enough so that Fargo could make out the words.

"You did a good job, Bitter Wind. You sure the girl you brought along ain't been touched?"

"My warriors left her alone except to make her ride and eat." The guttural voice had to belong to the leader of the war party. "Just as you said."

"Yeah, the boss was pretty firm about that. He may not be too happy that you only got one of the girls, though. He may want to pay you less than what you bargained for."

"Other girl here now," Bitter Wind protested.

"Yeah, but we're the ones who captured her, not you. It ain't fair for you to get the full price for deliverin' half the goods."

Bitter Wind's voice was as cold as his name as he said, "That is not for you to decide." Fargo sensed the tension in the air and hoped that a battle wouldn't erupt between the Comanches and their white allies. Jessie, Emily, or Whit might get in the way of a stray bullet if lead started flying around.

On the other hand, such a ruckus might provide enough of a distraction for Fargo to get the Franklins away from their captors—although as woozy as he still was from being knocked out, he wasn't sure how well he could function at the moment.

The tension eased as McCall said, "You're right, chief. That ain't up to me. You can hash it out later with the boss, after I've taken the girls to him."

"What about the other two?"

"Fargo and the boy?" McCall laughed. "I don't give a damn about them. I just brought 'em in to give to you as presents. Figured you might like to have some fun with the Trailsman. He'll probably take a long time to die."

"I have heard of this one called Fargo. He has fought my people before. My name will be honored if I take his hair."

"Well, go to it," McCall said. "Don't let me stop you. Although . . . it might be better if you waited until after we're gone in the mornin' to have your fun with him. I don't want the ladies bein' upset by what they might see, you know."

Surprisingly enough, McCall sounded like he was sincere about that. Fargo couldn't figure out why the man would be worried about whether Jessie and Emily were upset. But that wasn't the only thing McCall had said that Fargo couldn't quite figure out. The Comanchero had made several puzzling statements, such as his mention of some mysterious boss and his concern that Emily hadn't been molested during her captivity.

Bitter Wind must have thought over McCall's suggestion, because now the war chief said, "We will wait, as you ask. But tomorrow, when the sun rises . . . Fargo and the young one will die."

That was a break, Fargo thought. The longer the Comanches waited to kill him and Whit, the more time he would have to regain his strength and to figure out some way the two of them might escape and take Jessie and Emily with them. Sure, the chances of that were slim, but Fargo had beaten long odds plenty of times in the past, often with his life and the lives of others on the line.

He was pretty sure already from the things McCall had said that Jessie and Emily were still alive and unharmed. Now, as Bitter Wind pronounced his death sentence on Fargo and Whit, Jessie made her presence known by crying out angrily, "No! You can't do that."

McCall said, "You ain't in much of a position to be tellin' the chief what he can and can't do, missy. In case you ain't noticed, you and your sister are our prisoners."

"What do you want with us?"

"You'll find out in time."

Emily spoke up, saying, "What do you *think* they want with us?"

"Now, you're wrong about that, little missy," McCall said. "You think about it. Bitter Wind and his warriors ain't laid a finger on you, at least not like that, have they?"

"Well . . . no."

"You may not believe it, but you two gals are as safe right now as if you were sittin' in church. Nothin's gonna happen to you. You got my word on that."

Once again, Fargo was puzzled by McCall's apparent sincerity. He couldn't see any reason why the leader of the Comancheros would be so concerned about the well-being of the young women.

But McCall wasn't really the leader, Fargo reminded himself. He was taking orders from somebody else. The answers, if there were any answers to be had, would lie with that person.

A few feet away, Whit suddenly raised his head and groaned. He tried to push himself onto hands and knees as consciousness returned to him. He had to be acting instinctively, without any thought for what was going on around him. Before he could rise, one of the Comanches planted a foot in the middle of his back and shoved him down hard, driving his face into the dirt. The Indian put the barrel of a single-shot rifle against the back of Whit's head, causing both of his sisters to cry out in alarm.

Bitter Wind issued a sharp command. The Comanche with the rifle took it away from Whit's head and stepped back. Fargo eased his eyes closed again as McCall came over and hunkered in front of Whit.

"You don't want to be causin' trouble, young fella. Ol' Bitter Wind there is bein' generous. He's gonna let you and Fargo live until mornin'. But if you get rambunctious, he'll go ahead and kill you, and I won't do a damned thing to stop him."

"Who . . . who are you? How can you . . . cooperate with . . . these savages?"

"These savages, as you call 'em, are my business associates, boy. They been helpin' me get my hands on somethin' my boss wants. I'm talkin' about those sisters of yours."

"Why?" Emily cried. "Why does he want us? Did he send those Indians all the way to Lost Valley to kidnap us?"

"That's right," McCall said. "That's why Bitter Wind and his men had orders to bring you along, but not to hurt you. As for why the boss wants it that way . . ." The Comanchero leader paused, and even though Fargo's eyes were closed, he could almost see the man shrugging. "I couldn't tell you. You can ask him for yourself when we get where we're goin'."

"Where's that?"

"You'll see." McCall paused again, then went on. "Boy, I reckon you can sit up and visit with your sisters, seein' as how this is your last night and you'll never see 'em again after we ride out tomorrow mornin'. If you got anything you want to say, you better get 'er said."

Fargo heard Whit struggling to sit up. The young man asked, "Is Mr. Fargo all right?"

"He's just out cold." McCall chuckled. "I clouted him a good one with my pistol. He never saw it comin'."

That was true, Fargo thought. Despite his natural caution, McCall had fooled him.

"Come to think of it, though," McCall went on, "I figured he'd be awake by now. Larkin, get some water and throw it in his face."

Well, so much for pretending to be unconscious, Fargo thought. He had pulled it off for a while, and found out a few things. He maintained the pose until one of the Comancheros hooked a boot toe under his shoulder, rolled him onto his back, and dumped a bucket of water in his face. Then Fargo roused up sputtering and spitting, and he didn't have to pretend much, either.

McCall came over and slammed a rifle butt into Fargo's chest, driving him down onto his back again. McCall put the muzzle of the weapon about six inches from Fargo's nose.

"Welcome back to the land o' the livin', Fargo. Take a look around, and you'll see it won't do you no good to try to escape. You might as well take what you got comin' without raisin' a ruckus about it."

Fargo turned his head to look around. The members of the war party, as well as the Comancheros, were gathered around the pool. Most of them, red and white alike, were looking at Fargo with hatred and contempt. He had seldom felt such sheer hostility directed toward him. Any one of these men would kill him at a second's notice, on the slightest excuse.

"What's going on here?" he said, pretending a confusion he didn't feel. "McCall? What . . . what the hell happened?"

"You made a mighty big mistake takin' us for hide hunters and trustin' us, that's what happened," McCall said with a grin.

Jessie spoke up. "They're working with the Indians, Skye."

Fargo narrowed his eyes at McCall. "Comancheros?"

"That's right. If you've heard of us, you know there ain't any use in fightin'."

"What is it you want?"

"Those two gals. And before you start askin' me why, I don't know. The hombre I work for wants 'em, and he pays me good enough I don't ask any questions."

"What about Whit and me?"

"Hell, you know the answer to that! You ain't worth anything to me, so I'm gonna let Bitter Wind have you. He's the war chief o' these Comanch'. He's mighty excited about havin' the famous Trailsman to torture and kill."

McCall waved a hand toward one of the warriors as he spoke. Fargo glanced in the man's direction and saw that Bitter Wind was regarding him with a stony expression. If the war chief was excited, he wasn't showing it.

"Look, we can come to some sort of arrangement," Fargo began, knowing it wouldn't do any good. McCall probably expected him to try to bargain for his life, though.

"I've already come to an arrangement with the chief," McCall said with a shake of his head. "Forget it, Fargo. You'll be a dead man come mornin', and there's not a damned thing you can do about it."

Jessie began to sob quietly. Emily put an arm around her sister's shoulders and held her, comforting her even though Jessie was the older of the two.

"You're making a mistake, McCall," Fargo said. "The law will catch up to you sooner or later."

"All the way out here in Comancheria? Not damned likely! If there's ever any law in these parts, which I doubt, it's gonna be a hell of a long time in comin'."

McCall might be right about that, but Fargo doubted it. The dividing line between civilization and wilderness had been creeping steadily westward ever since the country had taken root, and he didn't expect that to change. Manifest destiny, the politicians called it. To Fargo, it was more a matter of human nature. Some fellas just had to push on out ahead of everybody else, and once they had extended the frontier, other folks always followed them, looking for fresh starts, new opportunities.

No, for good or bad, the way of life led by Bitter Wind and his people was doomed, more than likely. They just didn't know it yet.

And none of that would help him and Whit survive the next twelve hours, Fargo reflected.

McCall told a couple of his men to keep an eye on the prisoners, then went off to take a drink from a bottle of whiskey being passed around by some of the other Comancheros. The Indians began to ignore them as well.

The four captives sat together, Jessie and Emily huddling against each other. Jessie told Fargo what McCall had said earlier about the leader of the Comancheros making a deal with the Indians to raid the Franklin ranch and capture the sisters. Fargo nodded, not letting on that he had heard the same enigmatic statements from McCall.

"Do you have any idea who'd want to make an arrangement like that with the Comanches?" he asked.

Jessie shook her head. Emily and Whit did likewise.

"Skye, what are we going to do?" Jessie asked. Her voice trembled as if she were on the verge of losing control.

Fargo had been thinking about that. "Based on what's happened so far, I reckon McCall is telling the truth when he says that you two girls won't be hurt. You'll be safe enough if you go with him in the morning."

"And leave you and Whit to be killed?"

Fargo kept his voice pitched low enough so that none of their captors could hear him. "I don't intend to let that happen."

"How are you going to stop it?" Whit asked.

Fargo didn't lie. "I don't know . . . yet."

He sensed their disappointment with him, but there was nothing he could do about it right now. He figured that it would be better to wait until after the Comancheros left the next morning with Jessie and Emily before he and Whit made their move. Not only would the odds against them be that much less, but if there was any shooting, the young women wouldn't be around to maybe get in the way of a stray bullet.

Jessie, Emily, and Whit talked quietly among themselves, mostly things about home and their childhood. Fargo tried not to eavesdrop on these family matters, but he couldn't help overhearing some of the things they said. He was a little surprised when he realized from comments they made that Whit and the girls were only half siblings. Jessie and Emily had a different father. Whit's father had been kicked in the head by a mule when Whit was an infant and had died from the injury. A few years later, Grace had married a man named Henry Franklin, who had given Whit his name and been the only father the young man had ever known. In due time, Jessie and Emily had come along, and the family had been fairly happy on the ranch they established in Lost Valley, until Henry Franklin had gone out hunting one day with his brother Carl and fallen from a high bluff, breaking his neck. Evidently all three of the young people still had vivid memories of a weeping Carl Franklin bringing his brother's body home over the back of a horse. Grief-stricken, Grace had begged Carl to stay on at the ranch and help them run it, but her husband's younger brother had always been the shiftless sort who did everything in his power to avoid hard work. He had left not long after Henry's death, and they hadn't seen him since.

It was the sort of family history that was common on the frontier, full of tragedy and heartbreak, yet a stubborn persistence and pride had kept the Franklin family going. They had made a success of the ranch anyway.

Until the night of the Comanche raid.

With his head still aching from the blow McCall had struck, Fargo dozed off after a while. Most men facing death in a few hours wouldn't be able to sleep, but the Trailsman didn't intend to die. The Comanches hadn't tied him up, evidently feeling that he wouldn't try anything, surrounded by enemies as he was. Whit was loose, too. Their captors had taken Fargo's Colt and Arkansas toothpick, of course, but his Henry rifle was still in its sheath strapped to the Ovaro's saddle. Earlier, Fargo had studied the horses and Indian ponies being kept in a crude rope corral, and the Ovaro hadn't been among them. The stallion had gotten away, but Fargo felt confident that he was close by somewhere.

That was one good card Fargo had in the hand that had been dealt him. He just needed one or two more to take the pot. That was the thought in his head as sleep claimed him.

The sounds of men and horses moving around woke him. When he opened his eyes, he saw that the eastern sky was gray with the approach of dawn. The campfire had burned down during the night, but now one of the Indians stirred it up and soon had flames leaping from it again. That garish light revealed to Fargo that Jessie, Emily, and Whit had fallen asleep, too, their exhaustion proving too much to overcome. The three of them were slumped on the ground near him.

Luther McCall strode over, calling orders to his men to get the mules hitched up to the wagon. His loud voice woke the other three prisoners, who sat up rubbing their eyes. McCall grinned at them and asked, "You girls ready to take a little ride?"

"Go to hell!" Jessie said. Fargo admired her courage but questioned her wisdom.

McCall just laughed, though. "Say anything you want. Scream your head off, if that's what you want. There ain't anybody out here to care." He drew his gun. "Fargo, you and the boy move away from the gals now."

“No!” Whit said. “You can’t—”

“I can, and I’m gonna. Move, boy, or I’ll shoot you here and now so them sisters o’ yours have to watch you die.”

Fargo climbed to his feet and said, “Come on, Whit.”

“Damn it—”

Whit stopped his objection, stood up, and sighed in weary resignation.

McCall gestured with his revolver. “Go on around yonder, on the other side of the pool.”

Fargo and Whit walked around the water. Jessie and Emily began to sob. McCall tried to get them to eat or even drink some of the coffee that one of the Comancheros was brewing over the campfire, but they clung to each other and refused.

“All right,” McCall finally said in exasperation. “Load ’em in the wagon.”

The men moved in and grabbed Jessie and Emily. They fought back, writhing and struggling, but were no match for their captors’ superior strength. Being careful not to be too rough about it, the Comancheros wrestled them over to the wagon and lifted them into the back of it.

“You two stay there,” McCall told them. “I don’t want to have to tie your hands and feet, but if you jump outta that wagon even once, I’ll sure enough do it.”

Jessie looked at Fargo from eyes wide with horror. “Skye, do something!”

“Just cooperate with them for now, Jessie,” he told her. “And don’t lose hope.”

McCall laughed. “That’s big talk for a man who probably won’t be alive an hour from now. Or maybe you will, dependin’ on how long Bitter Wind wants it to take for you to die.” He swung up in his saddle. “Get that wagon rollin’!”

The Comancheros moved out. Jessie and Emily clung to each other, but they weren’t crying now. Instead, they each wore an expression of angry defiance.

McCall hung back. He grinned at the two remaining prisoners and lifted a hand in farewell.

"So long, Fargo. See you in hell."

With that, he rode away, too.

That left Fargo and Whit with the Comanches, who closed in around them. It was possible the Indians would just kill them out of hand, in which case the only thing the two white men could do against such overwhelming odds was to go down fighting. Fargo was betting their lives, though, that Bitter Wind would have something more elaborate in mind. Something more satisfying to his cruel nature.

The war chief made a curt gesture and spoke in his native tongue. Whit's face was pale and drawn with fear as he asked Fargo, "Do you know what he said?"

"He told the others to bring us along. We're going somewhere else."

"Where?"

Fargo shook his head. "The chief didn't say." A tight smile tugged at the Trailsman's mouth. "But however long it takes to get there, we'll be alive for that much longer, won't we?"

The Indians got on their ponies. They surrounded the prisoners and forced Fargo and Whit to march away from Buffalo Springs. Fargo's stomach was empty and his mouth was dry. The Comanches hadn't wasted any time giving breakfast to the two captives who were about to die. No point in wasting perfectly good food. Fargo didn't mind. Time enough to worry about that later, if he and Whit survived.

The sky grew brighter as they trudged along for the next half hour. The sun began to peek above the horizon, flooding the landscape with garish orange light. Fargo saw a dark line in front of them and realized it was a canyon that cut across the terrain. Such things weren't uncommon up here. Farther northwest, he knew, lay Palo Duro Canyon, which was large enough and spectacular enough to rival the giant canyon in northern Arizona Territory that Fargo had visited several times.

Whit saw the canyon, too. "Is that where we're goin'?"

The slash in the earth cut across in front of them as far as the eye could see in both directions. "It must be," Fargo said, "because I don't reckon we'll be going around it."

In a few more minutes, they were close enough to the canyon so that Fargo could see it was about a hundred yards wide. It was at least that deep, as well. He and Whit stopped before they got to it, but a couple of Comanches with lances prodded them ahead.

"Oh, God," Whit croaked. "They're gonna make us jump off that cliff."

That was what it looked like, all right, Fargo thought. The members of the war party surrounded them so that there was no way out.

Bitter Wind had something else in mind, though. He barked orders to his warriors, and several of them dismounted and came toward Fargo and Whit. Suddenly, they rushed in, grabbed the two prisoners, and tried to wrestle them to the ground.

Whit yelled and lashed out, struggling instinctively. Fargo fought in silence, slamming a fist into the jaw of one Comanche, making an unsuccessful grab for the sheathed knife on another's hip.

One of the Indians struck him on the side of the head and knocked him toward the canyon rim. Fargo caught himself before he plunged over the brink. He lowered his head and drove forward, tackling the warrior who had hit him. The man went over backward. Fargo stumbled and tried to keep his feet, but another of his captors brought clubbed fists down on his back, hammering him to the ground. A few feet away, Whit had been forced off his feet as well.

The odds were too great. Fargo and Whit couldn't stop the Comanches from tying them hand and foot with strips of rawhide. At least their hands were lashed together in front of them. That would give them a little more freedom, Fargo told himself. For whatever that was worth.

Ropes made of braided strips of rawhide were tied around their ankles and then made fast around some rocks that jutted up at the edge of the canyon. Then the Indians picked up both captives.

"Skye!" Whit cried. "Skye, what are they gonna do?"

Before Fargo had time to answer, the Comanches threw him and Whit over the brink. They sailed out into the canyon, with nothing underneath them but hundreds of feet of yawning death.

10

Whit let out a terrified scream. Fargo kept grimly silent. He knew what was going to happen.

Sure enough, a second later their plunge was halted by the ropes around their ankles. The hard jerk made pain shoot through Fargo's joints. Being brought up short like that caused him to swing back toward the cliff. He managed to twist around and get his hands in front of him to absorb some of the impact as he slammed against the rock. Even so, he hit the cliff with stunning force.

Off to his right, Whit crashed into the cliff, too, only he wasn't able to cushion the collision. He bounced off, then swung back and hit again. The way Whit's arms hung down limply told Fargo that he was unconscious.

Fargo twirled at the end of the rope. He closed his eyes so that the upside-down view and the spinning wouldn't make him sick. He put his hands out, felt them scrape against the rock. He grabbed on for whatever handhold he could get. Anything that might stabilize him a little would be welcome right now.

Above him, Bitter Wind called down, "Hang there like buffalo haunches until you die! You hear me, Fargo?"

Fargo didn't answer. He didn't want to give Bitter Wind the satisfaction.

Suddenly, he felt a little vibration in the rope tied around his ankles. That couldn't bode well. He had stopped spinning, so he risked opening his eyes and lifting his head so that he could look up at the top of the cliff. From this angle, he couldn't see Bitter Wind, but he could see the rising sun shining on a knife blade as the war chief knelt beside the rim and used the keen edge to saw at the rawhide rope.

Bitter Wind laughed. "Hang there as still as you can, Fargo, or the rope that I leave uncut will rub through on the rocks and snap. So you decide how long it will be before you die. Your fate is in your hands."

Of course it was. It always had been. Fargo's brain raced desperately as he searched for a way out of this deadly predicament.

Bitter Wind moved over and cut part of the way through Whit's rope as well. Now Whit being out cold was a good thing. He had stopped spinning and swaying for the most part. His limp form swung back and forth slightly in the wind that blew through the canyon, but the rope wasn't moving much. At that rate, it would take a while before it rubbed through on the sharp rocks that formed the rim.

"Good-bye, Fargo," Bitter Wind called. "Think of me while you wait to die."

I'm not liable to forget you, you son of a bitch, Fargo thought.

He waited there, staying as still as possible, until he heard the swift rataplan of hoofbeats as the Comanches climbed on their ponies and rode away. From down here, he couldn't tell if they had all left, or if Bitter Wind had left someone behind to keep an eye on them. Judging by the sound of the ponies, though, most, if not all, of the Comanches were gone.

Whit groaned.

Fargo grimaced and bit back a curse. He had an idea how to get out of this mess, but it would have helped if Whit had remained unconscious for a while longer. Now he had to worry about Whit coming to, panicking, and thrashing around until the rope supporting him wore through and parted.

"Whit!" Fargo said. "Whit, listen to me! You're all right! Whit!"

He looked over and saw the young man's eyelids fluttering. Whit opened his eyes a second later and immediately let out a yell of alarm.

"Whit! Damn it, listen to me! Stay as still as you can! Do you hear me, Whit?"

"Sk-Skye?" Whit managed to choke out. "What . . . where . . . Oh, I'm gonna be sick . . ."

"Just stay still," Fargo told him. "That's the most important thing you can do. You'll be all right, Whit. You're not going to fall. Just don't move around any more than you have to."

"All . . . all right. Skye, what . . . what are you gonna do?"

"Get us out of this," Fargo said.

He had found what he needed. About ten feet below him and just to his left, a roughly horizontal crack ran through the rocky face of the cliff. There were a lot of seams and cracks in the cliff, but that was the only one within reach. The crack was narrow, but wide enough that a man could get his fingers in it . . . if he could reach it.

There was only one way Fargo could do that.

He swung his arms so that his weight shifted. That rotated his body so that he was facing away from the cliff. Then he shifted his weight again. He began to swing from side to side, slowly at first, then a little faster. He thought he could hear the rope grating against the rock above him, but that was probably his imagination.

"Skye, what are you—"

"Don't talk. Just stay still."

Fargo continued swinging. He couldn't see the rope, so he couldn't tell how fast it was fraying. From the sound of Bitter Wind's mocking words earlier, the Comanche had cut most of the way through it. It shouldn't take much to snap it. Fargo knew he would have to react instantly when the rope snapped if he was going to have any chance of—

The rope gave a soft little *twang!* as it parted. Whit screamed, *"Skye!"*

Fargo didn't have time to think as he felt himself falling. Instinct took over instead, his muscles bunching, twisting his body, turning him toward the cliff as he reached out. His fingers scraped on the rock, then went into the crack. He dug in hard with them, knowing the terrible shock that was about to hit them.

The lower half of his body continued falling so that he was upright again for a split second before the weight threatened to jerk his fingers from their precarious grip. Fargo groaned as pain shot through his hands and made its wracking way up his arms and into his shoulders. His body struck the cliff face again.

He hung there, his fingers all that separated him from certain death.

His brain kept working, even through the pain and the dizziness and the instinctive fear he felt. The toes of his boots scrabbled against the cliff, searching for any slight protrusion that might support part of his weight. After a moment, he found one and dug the toes of his boots against it as hard as he could. That eased the awful strain on his fingers.

He rested his forehead against the rock and closed his eyes for a few seconds. Cold sweat bathed his face.

Gradually, he became aware that Whit was talking to him. "Skye, are you all right? Skye?"

Fargo took a deep breath. Not too deep, though, because he didn't want his expanding chest to push him away from the cliff face.

"Take it easy, Whit. We're going to be all right."

"You . . . you think you can climb out of here and pull me up?"

"That's the plan. Just be still, so you don't fray that rope holding you up."

Fargo lifted his head and looked up the cliff above him. Thirty feet had seldom seemed like such an overwhelming distance. He saw some handholds, though, if he could just reach them.

First he had to free his hands. He looked down the cliff face and found another little knob several inches above the one where his toes were lodged. Setting his grip with his hands even more firmly, he took his weight on them again and pulled his legs up so that his feet rested on that higher knob. From there, he was able to push himself up so that his head was on the same level as the crack where his fingers were hanging on for dear life.

Fargo leaned closer and started using his teeth to pull at the rawhide strips lashed around his wrists. The Comanches had done a good job on those bonds, pulling them cruelly tight, but Fargo worked with the desperation that came from knowing his life depended on what he was doing. He worked up enough spit to get the rawhide wet, and that helped it stretch and loosen a little.

It was a long, tedious job, made worse by the knowledge that no matter how still Whit managed to stay, the young man's weight was still going to work on that weakened rope holding him up. Fargo didn't have all day. He had to get his hands free before he could climb to the top of the cliff and save Whit.

Finally, the rawhide bonds were loose enough so that Fargo could work his right wrist out of them. He took that hand out of the crack and flexed the fingers to get the blood flowing better in them. Then he reached up for the next handhold.

Despite the urgency, Fargo knew he couldn't afford to rush. He had to be careful not to slip. Whit's life was riding on his efforts, as well as his own.

The fifteen minutes or so that it took Fargo to climb to the top was one of the longest quarter hours of his life. When he finally rolled over the rim, none of the Comanches were in sight. They had all departed, as he'd hoped. As he lay flat on his back with muscles trembling over his entire body, he wanted to just stay there and recover from the ordeal. But he knew he couldn't, so he turned onto his side and then scrambled onto hands and knees, heading for the rope from which Whit was suspended.

When he reached it, Fargo saw just how close the rope was to snapping. He sat with his feet braced against the rock that the rope was tied to, then grasped it firmly with both hands below the place where Bitter Wind had cut it.

"Hang on, Whit!" he called. "I'm going to pull you up."

There was no answer from below. Fargo wondered if Whit

had passed out again from hanging upside down like that for so long.

Pulling him up was easier said than done. Whit was so much deadweight, and Fargo's muscles were already exhausted from the climb. He began hauling back on the rope anyway. His progress was slow, a matter of a few inches at a time.

The sound of hoofbeats made him look around. Fargo's heart jumped when he saw the Ovaro approaching. Just as he had thought, the stallion had avoided capture by the Comanches but remained in the area, and now he was coming to rejoin the Trailsman.

Fargo whistled. The Ovaro broke into a trot at the summons and came to a stop next to Fargo, tossing his head happily at being reunited with his old friend. Fargo had a little extra rope now, since he had pulled Whit up a short distance, but not enough to tie to the saddle horn. Instead, he tightened his grip on the rope with his right hand and let go with his left. Reaching up quickly with that arm, he stuck it through the stirrup, crooking his elbow so that the stirrup caught it.

"Back up, boy! Back!"

The stallion began to back away from the canyon rim. Fargo kept his left elbow locked through the stirrup and hung on tight to the rope with his right hand. With the Ovaro's added strength, the task was easier and Whit rose faster. Fargo lifted himself from the ground and managed to get his left hand on the rope as well, while that arm was still through the stirrup. The Ovaro kept backing steadily.

After several feet, Fargo stopped the horse, reached as far down the rope as he could, held on tight, then sent the Ovaro ahead a few steps so he'd have some slack in the rope. He grabbed that slack with his left hand and dallied it around the saddle horn. Whit wouldn't fall now. Fargo got his arm loose from the stirrup and crawled back to the brink to look over it. Whit still dangled there, but he was only about ten feet below the rim now. Fargo told the Ovaro to back up again.

Within a few more minutes, Whit was close enough to the

top that Fargo was able to stretch out on his belly, reach down, and grab hold of the young man's feet. With the Ovaro's help, he pulled Whit the rest of the way out of the canyon. Fargo let the Ovaro drag Whit several yards from the edge before he called out to the stallion to stop.

Fargo went to the Ovaro, hopping because his ankles were still lashed together. He had a smaller knife in the saddlebags. He took it out and used the blade to cut the rope on his legs. He was a little shaky starting out, but his stride firmed up quickly as he returned to Whit's side. Kneeling beside the young man, he cut the ropes on Whit's wrists and ankles, freeing him.

Whit had passed out, all right. Fargo slapped his cheeks lightly, then fetched the canteen from his saddle when that didn't work. He lifted Whit's head and dribbled some water in his mouth. That got a reaction. Whit coughed and shook his head, then opened his eyes.

"Sk-Skye . . .? We're . . . alive?"

"You're damn right, we are," Fargo told him with a grin.

"How . . . how did you . . ."

"Never mind about that. What's important now is that we're out of that canyon, and we can start figuring out a way to go after your sisters."

Those words were barely out of Fargo's mouth when he heard a new sound that made him look up. More hoofbeats, this time from a lot of horses.

The Comanches coming back, or—

Fargo felt a wave of relief wash through him as he spotted the riders approaching the canyon. They wore blue uniforms, and riding at the head of the group were Lt. Kemp and Sgt. Monroe. Fargo wouldn't have thought that he'd ever be happy to see the young, glory-hungry officer and his brutal noncom again, but right now, that was the case.

Fargo stood up and waved to attract their attention, but the troopers had already spotted him and Whit and were coming straight toward them. Kemp held up a hand in the signal to halt. Monroe turned in his saddle and roared the order at the soldiers.

"Mr. Fargo," Kemp said. "I didn't expect to see you again. No doubt you didn't expect to see us, either, after you disobeyed my orders and fled the way you did." A worried frown suddenly creased the lieutenant's face. "Where's Miss Franklin?"

"The Comancheros have her."

Kemp looked confused. "You mean the Comanches?"

"No, the Comancheros. White outlaws who trade with the Comanches."

Kemp turned to look at Monroe. "Is he telling the truth, Sergeant?"

"About there bein' such a thing as Comancheros? Yeah, sure. I've heard of 'em. Used to be a lot of them up in the Panhandle and over in New Mexico Territory. Hasn't been much talk about them lately, though."

"They're back," Fargo said. "And they have both of the women now. That war party rendezvoused with a group of them and turned Emily Franklin over to them. They captured Jessie as well. My fault." His voice hardened. "So don't even think about telling me I'm not going with you to get them back."

"What makes you think I'm going after these so-called Comancheros?"

The question took Fargo by surprise. He frowned at Kemp and said, "What the hell do you mean by that?"

"My orders were to scout for and possibly engage with the Comanches. Nothing was said about . . . Comancheros. So unless they're still together . . . ?"

Fargo shook his head. "The Comancheros headed west with the girls. The war party went on north, I think."

"Then I'm sorry, but there's nothing I can—"

"Beggin' your pardon, Lieutenant," Monroe broke in. "I've been thinkin' about it, and nothin' gets a man noticed quite so quick out here as recoverin' white captives. I've got a feelin' the colonel might overlook it if you were to maybe not follow orders to the letter, especially if you saved a couple o' pretty young white gals from the Injuns and brought 'em back with you."

Kemp looked irritated at first, then intrigued. "You really think so, Sergeant?"

Monroe nodded solemnly. "I really do. I know the colonel, and I reckon he'd admire you for showin' some, what do you call it, initiative."

"Well, in that case . . . I suppose it wouldn't hurt to follow these . . . Comancheros . . . and find out what the situation is."

"I think you're makin' a smart decision, Lieutenant."

Fargo wasn't sure why Monroe had manipulated Kemp into going after the Comancheros. He suspected that it might have something to do with Jessie. Monroe might still want her for himself. If that was the case, he was going to be mighty disappointed. But regardless of the sergeant's motivation, Fargo knew he and Whit would have a better chance of freeing Jessie and Emily if they had the cavalry's help. The situation had changed from what it was before. If they could catch up to the Comancheros before McCall and the other outlaws got where they were going, they would have Jessie and Emily's captors outnumbered. Fargo knew that McCall's orders were to keep the two women safe and unharmed, too.

Of course, those had been Bitter Wind's orders, as well, but Fargo hadn't known that at the time.

The Henry was in the saddle boot, just as Fargo expected. "You wouldn't have an extra Colt I can borrow, would you?" he asked Kemp.

"I'm afraid not. We don't have an extra mount for young Franklin here, either."

"He can ride double with me. My stallion's strong enough to carry both of us, at least until we catch up to the Comancheros and get our other horses back."

"Do you think we can catch them today?"

"They're traveling with a wagon," Fargo explained. "We can move faster."

"Very well. By the way, Mr. Fargo, consider yourself under arrest, although I don't intend to have you restrained, of course."

Fargo glared at him. "Under arrest?"

"That's right. This entire region can be considered to be under martial law, and you disobeyed a direct order. Therefore, civilian or not, I have the authority to place you under arrest."

Fargo's eyes narrowed. "You've got some far-fetched notions, Lieutenant. But we can take that up once we get back to civilization with Jessie and Emily."

"Fine. Shall we go?"

Fargo swung up onto the Ovaro and reached down to give Whit a hand climbing onto the stallion's back behind him.

"I'll lead the way," he said.

Kemp didn't argue the matter.

The group moved out, backtracking the trail left by the Comanches when they brought Fargo and Whit to this canyon that had almost been the site of their deaths. When they reached Buffalo Springs, Kemp ordered his men to water the horses and fill their canteens.

"I didn't know this place was here," he told Fargo. "The terrain is rather arid, so I'm glad we have this chance to get water."

From there, the Comancheros' trail was easy to follow because the iron tires of the wagon left distinctive ruts in the dust. Fargo and Whit stayed out front on the Ovaro, with Kemp beside them and Sgt. Monroe just behind. Fargo didn't like having Monroe at his back. He didn't trust the sergeant. He didn't think Monroe would try anything with Kemp and the other troopers around, though.

The Comancheros didn't try to hide their tracks any more than their redskinned trading partners did. Fargo dismounted from time to time to study the droppings left by the horses and mules. He could tell from them that he and the cavalry patrol were cutting into the Comancheros' lead. At this rate, they would catch up before the day was over.

While they were stopped back at the springs, Fargo and Whit had drunk their fill from the pool, and the troopers had shared some jerky and hardtack with them. The food and water didn't make up for the grueling ordeal through which they had gone, but it helped make Fargo feel more human, anyway. As the sun rose higher in the sky and grew hotter, he missed the shade that his broad-brimmed Stetson usually provided. He could always get another hat, though, provided that he ever got back to civilization.

As they rode, Kemp asked Fargo about the strength of the group they were pursuing. "Do we simply engage the enemy?" he wanted to know. "Or do you think it would be advisable to pursue some other tactic?"

"That depends on what we find when we catch up to them," Fargo said. "If there's some place they can fort up, I reckon they could stand us off for a long time. You don't have enough men for that, Lieutenant. But if we can hit them out in the open, and hit them hard enough and fast enough, the fight ought to be over pretty quickly. And the quicker the better, as far as the prisoners are concerned. Less chance of them getting in the way of some flying lead."

"You said this man McCall was acting under the orders of someone else?"

"That's right. McCall's not the leader of the Comancheros. More like the Segundo. Second in command, to you, Lieutenant."

Kemp nodded. "Why would this mysterious employer of his go to so much trouble to have those two young women brought to him?"

"That's something we don't know yet." The more Fargo thought about it, the more that question puzzled him.

Midday came and went, and the heat built to a blistering level. They had to stop and rest the horses more often. Sweat lathered the sides of the animals and soaked the clothes of the men.

For a while, the trail had led toward a long ridge that angled from the northeast to the southwest. During one of the halts to rest the horses that afternoon, Fargo took the field glasses from his saddlebags and used them to study that ridge, being careful as usual not to let the sun reflect off the lenses.

"There's something up there," he murmured as Whit stood

beside him. "Some sort of canyon that opens into that escarpment . . ."

"Do you think that's where they're going?"

"Could be. The trail seems to lead straight toward the gap."

As they pushed on and drew closer to the ridge, Fargo's instincts told him the canyon he had seen was their destination. He said to Kemp, "Lieutenant, I think your men should wait here while I go on ahead to check out the lay of the land."

"You're not going without me, Mr. Fargo," Kemp said. "You're under arrest, remember?"

Fargo felt a surge of irritation. "What do you think I'm going to do, run away? I just want to get an idea of what we're up against."

"That's an excellent idea. I'll go with you."

Whit said, "So will I. That's my sisters those bastards carried off."

Fargo saw that arguing was going to waste more time than it was worth. He nodded and said, "All right. Have one of your men loan Whit a horse, Lieutenant, in case we have to get back here in a hurry."

Kemp hesitated, then nodded. "All right. That makes sense."

A few minutes later, while Monroe and the rest of the troopers stayed behind, Fargo, Whit, and Kemp continued on the trail of the Comancheros. Fargo urged the Ovaro into a fast lope. He had a feeling it might be a good idea to get closer before their quarry had a chance to disappear into that canyon.

Twenty minutes later, they came to a stop on a small, brushy hill that gave them a good view of the ridge and the canyon that cut into it. Fargo told his companions to dismount. They tied their reins to mesquite trees, and Fargo led the way up the hill on foot.

When they reached the top, they stretched out and Fargo brought the field glasses to his eyes again. Training them on the mouth of the canyon, he muttered a surprised exclamation.

"What is it?" Kemp asked.

"Do you see the Comancheros, Skye?" Whit wanted to know. "Can you see Jessie and Emily?"

Fargo shifted the glasses, then stopped as the wagon leaped into view through the lenses. "Yeah, I see them. They're all right, Whit. The Comancheros are headed for a house in the mouth of that canyon."

"A house?" Kemp repeated in surprise. "Out here?"

"More like a hacienda," Fargo said. He moved the glasses again. "Lord knows how old it is. I'd guess close to a hundred years, though. Some Spanish grandee from New Mexico Territory must've gotten the idea of coming over here and starting a ranch. He built himself a big, fancy house . . . and then the Comanches must've killed him or sent him running for home. The place looks like it's been abandoned for years."

"Then why are the Comancheros going there?"

"Because they've moved in and made it their headquarters, I'd guess," Fargo replied. "I see some horses in a corral that looks like it's been rebuilt recently. I reckon the leader of the gang and a few of his men stayed here while McCall and the rest of the bunch rendezvoused with Bitter Wind."

Fargo studied the hacienda through the glasses again. Despite the air of run-down abandonment about the place, it was still impressive, a sprawling adobe house in the Spanish style, with a roof made of red tile that had probably been brought from Santa Fe by wagon.

McCall's bunch was still about a quarter of a mile from the house in the mouth of the canyon when someone shoved open the heavy front door and stepped outside. The man swaggered out and waited for the newcomers. Fargo focused the glasses on him. He was big and broad-shouldered, with a craggy face under a broad-brimmed black hat with silver conchos on the band. A sandy mustache drooped over his mouth. He wore a black vest and black sleeve protectors on his wrists. The butt of an ivory-handled revolver jutted up from a black holster on his hip. Despite looking a little like a dandy, the man had a definite air of menace about him, and it came clearly through the field glasses as Fargo watched him. Fargo's instincts told him that he was looking at the leader of the Comancheros.

"Take a look at the man standing in front of the house," Fargo said as he handed the field glasses to Whit. "See if you recognize him."

Whit took the glasses. He handled them a little awkwardly as he tried to locate the man Fargo was talking about. Fargo knew when he did, though, because Whit suddenly caught his breath and then said, *"Son of a bitch!"*

"You know him?"

"You're damned right I do." Whit looked over at Fargo with shocked eyes. "That's my uncle Carl!"

11

Well, that explained a few things, Fargo thought. Not all of them, but it was a start, anyway.

"That's why he didn't want the girls hurt. He's related to them."

Whit handed the field glasses back to Fargo with an amazed shake of his head. "Yeah, but how did a shiftless no-account like Uncle Carl ever wind up bossin' a bad outfit like these Comancheros? Ma had a soft spot for him, since he was Pa's brother, but everybody else knew what he was really like."

"People change," Fargo said. "Something must've happened to him to toughen him up."

The wagon had rolled to a stop in front of the hacienda. As Fargo watched, some of McCall's men lifted Jessie and Emily out of the vehicle and wrestled them over in front of Carl Franklin. Even from this distance, Fargo could see the shocked surprise both young women felt at the sight of their uncle. Franklin stepped up to Jessie and tried to hug her.

She slapped him across the face.

Franklin drew back, and for a second, Fargo thought the man was going to strike Jessie in return. But then he just shook his head and said something, then gestured toward the hacienda. McCall's men took hold of Jessie and Emily and steered them into the big, old house.

"What's going on now?" Whit asked anxiously.

"They're taking the girls inside," Fargo told him. "Looked like your uncle tried to talk to them, but Jessie slapped him."

"Yeah, that sounds just like something she'd do. She got

along with Carl all right while he was stayin' with us, but I don't think she ever really liked him. None of us did."

Lt. Kemp had brought along his own pair of field glasses. He studied the hacienda through them and then asked, "What do you suggest we do now, Mr. Fargo, since we weren't able to catch up to the Comancheros before they reached their headquarters?"

"The walls of that house are thick. It was built to withstand an attack. So we can't come at them head-on. We'll have to wait for nightfall and then come up with some sort of distraction, so we can hit them from two directions at once."

Kemp nodded. "Those are sound tactics."

Whit said, "I don't like how we have to keep waitin', Skye."

"We're still alive, aren't we?" Fargo pointed out. "We've got the element of surprise on our side now, Whit. McCall thinks that you and I are dead, and unless Jessie said something about it, he doesn't even know that there's a cavalry patrol out here in this area. That bunch down there won't be expecting any trouble . . . but we're going to give it to them anyway."

Fargo grinned as he made that last statement.

"All right," Whit agreed. "You got us out of that canyon when I thought for sure we were both dead, so I reckon I'll string along with you, Skye."

The three men mounted up and rode back to rejoin the rest of the patrol. Kemp explained the situation to Sgt. Monroe. The burly noncom thought it over and then said, "Seems to me that me and the boys ought to make a feint at the front of the place while you and Fargo and the kid go in the back and get those gals."

"That's exactly what I was thinking, Sergeant," Kemp said, although Fargo doubted if that plan really had occurred to the lieutenant before now. "The safety of the women is paramount. Once we've rescued them, we can lay siege to the place and root those Comancheros out at our leisure." Kemp turned to the Trailsman. "What do you think, Mr. Fargo?"

"I had in mind something along those lines as well," Fargo said. He had been debating whether to take Kemp with him and Whit but was leaning that way, thinking it might be better to have the lieutenant where he could keep an eye on him. He still didn't trust Monroe, but at least the sergeant had some experience when it came to a fight.

Kemp nodded. "It's settled, then. You and Mr. Franklin and I will circle around and approach the Comancheros' headquarters from the rear. Sergeant, you'll give us an hour to get in position, then lead the troop in a frontal assault on the enemy stronghold. Pull back when the return fire becomes heavy, though. We don't want to throw away any lives needlessly."

"Yes, sir," Monroe said.

"That means all we have to do now is wait for nightfall. It's still several hours away, isn't it?"

"That's right," Fargo said.

And knowing that Jessie and Emily were in there was going to make the wait seem even longer.

During the next few hours, the men rested and ate, while Fargo and Kemp discussed their plans. Kemp agreed to let Fargo penetrate the Comanchero stronghold alone, while he and Whit waited outside to provide covering fire if need be when Fargo brought out Jessie and Emily.

The ridge caused the hacienda to be cast in shadow before the sun was all the way down. Watching from the hilltop, Fargo saw lights flare inside the old dwelling. He waited until the fiery red orb dropped completely behind the ridge before he returned to the others and told Kemp and Whit, "Let's go."

Once again, they took one of the cavalry horses for Whit to ride. Fargo planned to stampede the animals in the corral to slow down possible pursuit, and while he was at it, he figured he would grab a couple of mounts for Jessie and Emily as well.

With shadows forming, Fargo figured that any lookouts posted by the Comancheros wouldn't be able to spot him and his two companions, but he led them in a wide circle around the place, anyway, just to be careful. They had come too far and endured too much to fail now. They reached the ridge a good half mile northeast of the hacienda, where they climbed to the top of it and then started back toward the canyon. Like the Cap Rock escarpment farther west and the Balcones down in central Texas, this one was almost perfectly flat on top and not hard to climb because of the erosion that had eaten away at it over the centuries.

By the time they reached the canyon, the sky was almost completely dark. Stars had begun to come to life in the heavens. The darkness made the lights in and around the hacienda seem even brighter. Several torches had been lit outside and cast flickering glares around the place. Fargo grimaced when he saw that, because the torches would make approaching the hacienda that much more difficult.

As he studied the layout, though, he saw some cover he could use—the corral with the horses inside it, an old barn, a couple of outbuildings where the roofs had collapsed with age and disuse. He thought he could get close enough to risk a dash into the house. Once he was there, he would still have to find and free Jessie and Emily, but he couldn't make any advance plans for that. Getting inside was the first step.

"We'll get down there behind that barn," Fargo told Whit and Kemp. "The two of you will wait there with the horses. Lieutenant, I'll need your revolver. If I run into any trouble, chances are it'll be at close quarters, where a handgun will be better than a rifle."

Kemp agreed with the suggestion this time. He drew his Colt and handed it to Fargo, who slipped it into the empty holster on his hip. He gave the Henry to the lieutenant. Whit had a rifle he had borrowed from one of the cavalry troopers.

Fargo explained his plan to stampede the Comancheros' horses. "Then we'll head back to the top of the ridge and ride like hell. I'm hoping that by the time we rendezvous with the rest of the patrol, we'll have a good lead on anybody who tries to come after us."

The walls of the canyon sloped gently enough so that they

were able to lead the horses down them. All of Fargo's senses were keenly alert as he searched for any sign of a sentry behind the hacienda. He didn't believe the Comancheros would be so confident that they wouldn't bother to post any guards, but he also hoped they might not be too watchful. They probably thought they didn't have any real enemies within a hundred miles.

When they reached the old adobe barn, they hid in the deep shadows behind it. Fargo said in a half whisper, "Now we wait for Sergeant Monroe and the rest of the patrol to start that distraction."

Fargo figured that almost an hour had passed since they left Monroe and the troopers, so they shouldn't have long to wait. Time stretched by, though, and the night was still quiet and peaceful, with no shots from the other side of the hacienda. The only sounds that Fargo heard, in fact, were the horses moving around in the corral, the cry of a nightbird, and the notes of a guitar as someone inside the big house strummed it.

"Hasn't it been long enough?" Whit finally asked.

Fargo gave a grim nod. When he realized that Whit probably couldn't see him, he said, "Yeah. Something must have happened to delay them."

"What could that be?" Kemp asked. "We didn't hear any shooting, either here at the hacienda or out there where we left them."

"I don't know. But it doesn't look like they're coming."

"What are we gonna do?" Whit said. "We can't just leave Jessie and Emily in there, even if Uncle Carl really *is* the leader of those outlaws."

"We're not going to leave them in there," Fargo promised. He reached a decision. "I'm going to go find them right now."

"Even without the distraction?" Kemp asked.

"Even without the distraction. Maybe I can get in and out without anybody seeing me."

Fargo knew just what a long shot that possibility was, but

he had a bad feeling about that cavalry patrol. If a Comanche war party had stumbled on them, there should have been some shooting, but even though Fargo couldn't explain why they hadn't shown up, he had a hunch they weren't coming.

He reached out in the darkness, squeezed Whit's shoulder reassuringly, then slid out from behind the barn and moved in a crouch toward the hacienda, using the horses in the corral to shield him from view.

He stopped at the corner of the corral to check the house for any sign that he'd been spotted. Nothing had changed, so he darted across an open space to one of the tumbledown old outbuildings. From there, he repeated the dash to the next ruin and then ran to the corner of the house, ducking into some shadows.

Everything was still quiet. Fargo glanced toward the barn where he'd left Whit and Kemp. He didn't know if they could see him or not. He figured they were getting pretty nervous by now.

He grinned tightly in the darkness. His nerves were drawn a mite taut, too.

The hacienda had two stories, with a balcony overhanging a porch that appeared to go all around the house. Fargo catfooted over to one of the pillars that supported the balcony and began climbing it. It was made from a thick wooden beam, but he was able to wrap his arms and legs around it and shinny up as if it were a tree. When he got to the top, he reached up and grasped the wrought-iron railing that went along the edge of the balcony.

With only a slight grunt of effort, Fargo pulled himself up and over the railing. That wasn't nearly as hard as climbing out of that other canyon had been, early that morning. He had chosen a spot where the windows of the rooms along the balcony were dark, but farther along, yellow glows spilled through some of the other windows. Fargo eased toward them.

Any curtains that had hung over the windows had long since rotted away. The first room Fargo came to was empty.

The light inside came through a door into a hallway. The second room was the same. The light in the window of the third room was brighter, though, so Fargo had a feeling there was a lamp in there. And where there was a lamp, there were probably people.

He pressed his back against the wall and slid along it until he could edge an eye past the side of the window and look into the room. When he did, his heart slugged in his chest. Jessie and Emily were in there, sitting at a table and looking disconsolate.

Luther McCall was in the room, too, sitting in a chair near the door. He had the chair tipped back so that it stood on its rear legs. He rocked it back and forth lazily. Clearly, he was here to keep an eye on the girls and make sure that they didn't escape through the window.

Fargo drew back slightly from the window and eased the borrowed Colt from his holster. He needed to lure McCall over to the window some way so he could knock him out. Once that was done, it would be simple for Jessie and Emily to climb out the window and escape with him.

Sections of the adobe wall had crumbled and pieces had broken off in places. Fargo picked up one of the chunks of rubble and tossed it along the balcony on the other side of the window. When McCall stuck his head out to see what the noise was, Fargo wanted the Comanchero's head turned away from him.

McCall bit on the bait. Fargo heard the chair's front legs thump onto the floor as McCall sat up.

"What the hell was that?" McCall muttered. Heavy footsteps approached the window.

Fargo lifted the Colt and poised it over his head, ready to strike swiftly and silently.

Instead of leaning forward to peer out the window in the other direction, though, McCall thrust his gun through the opening and trained it on Fargo. A grin creased the outlaw's beard-stubbled face.

"'Bout time you showed up, Fargo," McCall said.

Fargo was ready to leap aside and trade shots with the man if he had to, but before he could move, he heard more guns being cocked behind him. A bitter, sour taste formed under his tongue as he realized that McCall wasn't the one who had taken the bait.

He was.

"Drop the gun, Fargo," a voice called. A fresh shock went through the Trailsman as he recognized it.

He turned his head and saw that several men had come around the corner on the balcony and now had revolvers and rifles pointed at him. Among them were Carl Franklin, the leader of the Comancheros . . .

And Sgt. Pike Monroe of the United States Cavalry.

The noncom grinned at him and said, "Didn't expect to see me here, did you, Fargo? There's no use waiting for the rest of the patrol, either. They're all locked up downstairs."

Carl Franklin swaggered forward, the ivory-handled gun in his hand pointed indolently at Fargo. "You were told to drop that gun, mister. You'd better do it, unless you want to die right here and now."

Slowly, with a grim look on his face, Fargo lowered the Colt. McCall reached out and took it from his hand, then pulled his head and shoulders back into the room where Jessie and Emily were being held prisoner.

"That's better," Franklin said.

Jessie pushed past McCall to the window. "Skye! You're alive! I knew you'd come for us." With a bitter twist, she added, "But now they have you, too. I swear, Emily and I didn't know they were setting a trap for you. We didn't even know you were still alive."

Fargo nodded and smiled faintly at her. "I never thought that, Jessie."

"Step away from that girl, Fargo," Franklin said. "I don't want you anywhere near Jessie and Emily, in case we have to shoot you."

"Mighty protective of them, aren't you?"

"Why shouldn't I be? They're my daughters."

And that was the last piece in the puzzle, Fargo thought. Grace Franklin had married one brother, but the other brother was the father of her younger children. Whit had mentioned that his mother had had a soft spot for Carl Franklin. He just hadn't known how friendly they'd really been.

"What did you do, finally decide that you wanted them with you again?"

"You're not in any position to be askin' questions . . . but yeah, that's about it. The first few years after I left the ranch, I didn't have a nickel to my name. I couldn't have provided for any young'uns. It took me this long to finally make somethin' of myself."

"An outlaw," Fargo said. "A Comanchero."

Franklin sneered. "A rich man. That's what I am."

From the window, Jessie said, "I still don't believe it. I don't care what you say. If you really cared about us, you could have stayed in Lost Valley. Mama wanted you to."

"And be tied down to a life of hard work on a greasy sack outfit like Henry's?" Franklin shook his head. "That wasn't for me, gal. But I never forgot about you and your sister. Not ever."

"I've said it before, and I'll say it again . . . Go to hell."

Franklin's craggy face hardened. "I'm sorry you feel that way, gal. I reckon I'll have to teach you and your sister to respect your pa, whether you want to or not." He turned to the men with him. "Some of you go out and bring in the boy and that shavetail lieutenant Monroe told us about."

As several of the Comancheros hurried away to carry out Franklin's orders, Fargo looked at Monroe and said, "What did you do, lead the rest of the patrol right into a trap?"

Monroe grinned. "Damn right I did. I've had my fill of the army. I'm ready to make some real money, and I figure these Comanchero fellas have a good deal worked out. I told the troop I was gonna scout out ahead, and then I found one of the sentries and had him take me to see the boss."

Franklin took up the tale. "Once Pike convinced me he really wanted to join up with us, we worked out a deal. With his help, we captured those troopers without firin' a shot. When Bitter Wind shows up tomorrow with his whole band, he'll be happy to have a whole heap of white soldier boys to torture and kill."

"The Comanches are coming here?"

"That's right. We're havin' a little fandango for them, and they're bringin' us a mess of slaves to take to Mexico. Maybe I'll spare Whit's life, seein' as how he's almost family, and take him to Mexico and sell him, too."

From the window, Jessie said, "You son of a bitch!"

"We may have to beat that stubborn streak outta you yet, girl," Franklin said. "Luther."

McCall pushed Jessie aside and stuck his head out the window. "Yeah, boss?"

"Take Fargo and my daughters downstairs and lock 'em up in that old pantry. We'll put Whit and the lieutenant in there, too, when the other boys bring them in."

Monroe said, "I want—" Then he stopped short. Fargo figured he'd been able to say something about wanting Jessie for himself, then remembered that Carl Franklin was her father. That hope probably still lurked in Monroe's brutal mind, but he would have to bide his time.

If Carl Franklin was smart, he wouldn't trust Monroe too far, that was for sure. A man who would betray his fellow soldiers would betray anybody.

Franklin gestured with the gun in his hand. "Come on, Fargo."

For a second, Fargo considered the odds of vaulting over the balcony railing and getting away. With three or four guns trained on him, they were pretty small, he decided. Even if he made it over the rail, he might break a leg on landing, and Jessie and Emily would still be in the hands of the Comancheros.

With a curt nod, Fargo followed Franklin's orders. His captors marched him around the corner, where they met McCall coming through a door with Jessie and Emily in front of him. The whole group moved along the balcony to the next corner, where some stairs led down to the ground. Then Franklin, McCall, and the others prodded the three captives into the old house, where they were taken to a small, empty room adjacent to the kitchen. This room had a door on it that still looked fairly sturdy.

"There'll be guards right out here the rest of the night," Franklin told the prisoners. "So don't get any fancy ideas, Fargo. I want to turn you over to Bitter Wind while you're still alive, so I can see the look of surprise on that red-skinned face of his. But I'll settle for showing him your corpse if I have to."

Fargo didn't say anything. He just went inside the old pantry with Jessie and Emily. The door closed solidly behind them.

The room had one small window, high in the back wall. The shutter that had once been over it was long since rotted away, but the opening was too narrow for any of them to get through it, even Emily, who was the smallest of the three prisoners. The window let in a little fresh air, though, as well as some reflected glow from the torches that burned outside the hacienda.

As soon as they were alone, Jessie threw her arms around Fargo and hugged him tightly. "I thought you were dead," she whispered. "McCall kept talking about how that Comanche war chief was going to kill you."

"Old Bitter Wind came close," Fargo said. "Whit and I made it out alive, though."

Emily came up to him and tentatively slipped her arms around him, too. "Jessie told me how you wouldn't give up on finding me and rescuing me, Mr. Fargo. And how you risked your life to do it. Thank you for trying . . . even if it didn't work out."

"Don't give up yet," Fargo told her. "We're just waiting for our chance to turn the tables on your father and his men."

Jessie stepped back and gave a vehement shake of her head. "Carl's *not* our father. I don't care what he says. I'll never believe him."

Fargo didn't say anything. He had no doubt that Franklin

had been telling the truth about the girls being his daughters, but if Jessie and Emily didn't want to believe it, that was their business.

Might make things easier that way, in fact, because Fargo planned to kill Carl Franklin, sooner or later.

12

Fargo expected the Comancheros to show up shortly with Whit and Lt. Kemp as their prisoners, but as the night dragged on, no one opened the door. Jessie noticed that, too, and asked Fargo, "Do you think they could have gotten away?"

That seemed unlikely to Fargo, given the relative inexperience of both men. It was more likely they had put up a fight and had been killed.

But he didn't want to say that to Jessie and Emily, so he just said, "Could be. If they did, maybe they can do something to help us get away from these varmints and settle the score with them."

Jessie frowned. "Whit? And the lieutenant?"

"Sometimes when a fella's back is to the wall, he can accomplish more than even he thought was possible," Fargo said with a smile.

Exhaustion and the strain of the past few days took its inevitable toll. Both young women went to sleep, and after a while Fargo dozed off, too, with Jessie leaning against him and resting her head on his shoulder.

When he woke up sometime later, the light in the makeshift cell had faded to the faint glow of the stars coming through the little window. The torches outside had either gone out or been extinguished.

He didn't need to see, though, to know what was going on. Jessie had straddled his lap and was now working at the buttons on his buckskins, trying to free the shaft that she had rubbed into hardness through his clothing.

Fargo slid a hand behind her neck, cupping it as he brought

her face to his and kissed her. After a moment, he pulled back and whispered, "What about Emily?"

"She's sound asleep," Jessie replied. And it was true that Fargo could hear the younger woman's deep, regular breathing a few feet away. "If we're quiet, we won't wake her up."

Fargo wasn't sure that was going to be possible, but since Jessie had succeeded in freeing his manhood and now wrapped both soft hands around the long, thick pole, he figured it was worth a try.

She had slipped off her riding skirt, so as she moved closer to him, she was able to bring his member to her already-wet opening and then sink down on it slowly. Fargo clenched his jaw to keep from groaning in pleasure as he felt the heated slickness enveloping him. He put his hands on Jessie's hips to steady her as she sheathed him deeper and deeper within her.

Once he was lodged fully inside her, she began rocking her hips back and forth. Fargo met those little thrusts with surges of his own. Jessie put her arms around Fargo's neck and leaned in to kiss him again. Her lips parted as his tongue probed against them and then slid into her mouth.

It was long, slow, languorous lovemaking they shared there in the darkness, with a bittersweet quality all its own. Fargo knew that Jessie had given up hope. This was her way of saying good-bye to him. She thought that come morning, she would have to watch him being turned over to Bitter Wind for the second time, and surely this time the Comanche war chief wouldn't leave even the slightest opening for Fargo to escape.

Fargo wasn't ready to surrender just yet, though. He would go down fighting if he had to, but deep inside him burned the belief that somehow, he would find a way out of this.

For one thing, the Comancheros still hadn't brought in Whit and Lt. Kemp. They might still be alive. If that was true, Fargo didn't believe that Whit would run away without at least trying to rescue his sisters. If he and the lieutenant could stage some sort of distraction . . . if Fargo could manage to free the cavalry troopers and get some guns in their hands . . . if he could get one shot at Carl Franklin and Luther McCall and Pike Monroe . . .

That was a lot of *ifs*. But Fargo couldn't banish them from his mind, any more than he could have refused Jessie the pleasure they both now shared. He flexed his hips, driving his erect shaft in and out of her hot, wet core, feeling the tension building in her muscles as he stroked her back, until finally she began to shudder as her culmination washed over her.

Fargo let go as well, holding her tightly as he emptied himself in a series of throbbing eruptions. When the spasms finally eased for both of them, they slumped against each other. Jessie was breathing hard, but that was the loudest sound either of them had made. A few feet away, Emily continued to slumber soundly, at least as far as the Trailsman could tell.

When Jessie was able to lift her head again, she brushed her lips across Fargo's cheek in a kiss that was tender, almost chaste, even. Fargo returned it by kissing her forehead. Then they put their arms around each other and held on tightly.

"Don't give up," Fargo whispered in her ear. "Don't ever give up."

"I . . . I'll try not to. But it seems so hopeless."

"Not as long as we're still alive," Fargo said. "Not as long as we can fight. We just need a little luck."

"Or a miracle," Jessie said.

Fargo smiled in the darkness. "I'd take that, too," he said.

Jessie pulled her clothes back on and sat down beside him again. They dozed off as they leaned against each other, and Fargo didn't wake up until the bright sunlight of morning had begun to slant through the little window above their heads. He had slept considerably later than he normally did.

Jessie still leaned against him and slept, but Emily was awake, sitting up with her back against the wall a few feet away. She looked at him and said, "Jessie really likes you, you know, Mr. Fargo."

"And I like her," Fargo said. "I think she's a fine girl."

"But if we somehow do manage to get out of this alive, that won't stop you from riding away and breaking her heart, will it?"

"I've never been the sort of hombre to stay in one place for too long," Fargo admitted.

"I didn't think so." Emily sighed. "Still, I can't blame her, I suppose. Or you."

She didn't say anything else, but that was enough to make Fargo wonder if she hadn't been quite as sound asleep as she had seemed to be the night before.

He didn't wonder for long, though, because a few minutes later, the door opened and McCall stepped into the room, gun in hand. "All right, you three," he said. "On your feet. Bitter Wind and his people are comin' in."

Jessie woke up, looked around, and then glared at McCall. "Where's my brother?"

McCall didn't answer the question. "I said get up." He reached down with his free hand to grab her arm.

That brought him within reach of Fargo, who surged up from the floor and slammed a fist into McCall's face, at the same time using his other hand to bat the Comanchero's gun aside. The Colt blasted, but the bullet went harmlessly into the wall.

Fargo slugged McCall again, knocking him back into another guard who came rushing into the room in response to the shot. Their legs tangled up and caused both men to fall. Fargo kicked the guard in the jaw, breaking the bone and knocking him senseless. He twisted the Colt out of McCall's stunned fingers and brought the butt of the weapon across the man's face in a slashing blow that pulped McCall's nose and made blood spurt from it.

McCall still had plenty of fight left in him, though. He came up from the floor with a knife in his hand that he'd jerked from behind his belt. In the brief glimpse of the blade Fargo got, he recognized his own Arkansas toothpick. He had to leap backward to avoid being gutted.

He was dimly aware of gunfire going on outside, the popping of handguns and the sharper cracks of rifles. He wasn't sure what was going on, but he was thankful for the ruckus. Nobody else seemed to be paying any attention to the single shot that had come from the old pantry.

Snarling curses, McCall leaped at Fargo again and thrust the knife toward the Trailsman's throat. Fargo turned it aside with the gun in his hand, steel ringing on steel as he did so. While McCall was a little off balance, Fargo sunk a fist in his belly. As McCall doubled over in pain, Fargo brought up his knee. It caught McCall in the face and threw him backward. He fell through the open door and rolled across the hallway outside the pantry.

When he pushed himself up, his hands were empty. He looked down at his belly and saw the handle of the Arkansas toothpick protruding from it. Crimson welled out around the blade that was buried deep in McCall's guts. He managed to croak, "Damn you . . . Fargo . . ." before his eyes rolled up in their sockets and he fell forward on his face. That just drove the knife deeper, but McCall didn't feel it anymore.

Fargo glanced at Jessie and Emily. They both still sat there, looking stunned by the sudden outbreak of violence. Fargo hadn't planned this, but he had seen his opportunity and seized it.

Fargo rolled McCall's corpse onto its back, pulled out the knife, and wiped the blood off the blade on McCall's shirt. He slid the toothpick back into its sheath on his leg, where it belonged.

The guard whose jaw he had broken was armed with a rifle and a handgun. Fargo took both weapons, handed the pistol to Emily and the rifle to Jessie. He punched extra cartridges from the loops on the shell belts worn by McCall and the unconscious guard and divided them among the three of them.

"Skye, what are we going to do?" Jessie asked.

"Try to get our hands on some horses and stampede the rest of the mounts. Then we'll make a run for it."

McCall had said that Bitter Wind and the rest of the Comanches had arrived at the Comanchero stronghold, though, which meant the Indians would probably give chase, even if

Fargo and the girls managed to grab some horses. The odds against their survival were still mighty long.

But they were armed and had a fighting chance now. For the moment, Fargo would take that.

He led the two young women into the hallway, looking both directions to make sure no one was in sight. Amazingly enough, this part of the hacienda seemed to be deserted.

That was because everyone was outside, Fargo saw when they came to a window, getting started on that fandango Carl Franklin had promised Bitter Wind. He saw Comancheros and Comanches mingling together outside, drinking and firing their guns into the air in celebration. Exactly what they were celebrating, Fargo didn't know. They probably didn't need much of a reason.

He spotted Bitter Wind talking to Carl Franklin and Pike Monroe. The Comanche war chief didn't seem too happy about having a cavalryman there, judging by the way he kept glaring at Monroe, but evidently Franklin had vouched for the sergeant.

Fargo motioned for Jessie and Emily to stay back away from the window. "Careful," he whispered. "We don't want them to spot us. Let's head for the back and try to make it to the corral."

Gun in hand, he led the way, hoping that Franklin wouldn't get impatient for McCall to return with the prisoners and come looking for them, at least not for a while. As they approached the rear of the hacienda, Fargo suddenly heard footsteps ahead of them, around a corner. He waved Jessie and Emily back and leveled the Colt.

The unshaven hardcase who stepped around the corner was one of the Comancheros who had been with McCall, the men Fargo had mistaken for hide hunters. He stopped short at the sight of Fargo and the two women, his eyes widening in surprise. He clawed at the pistol on his hip and opened his whiskery mouth to yell.

Fargo leaped forward. His left hand closed around the man's throat, shutting off any outcry, and at the same time his right brought the gun down hard on the man's head. The high-crowned Stetson absorbed some of the blow's force, but not enough to keep it from driving the man to his knees. Fargo hit him again and this time heard bone crunch under the impact. The Comanchero slumped limply against the wall, probably already dying from his shattered skull. Fargo let him fall to the floor.

"Is . . . is he dead?" Emily asked.

"Soon will be."

"Good riddance," Jessie said.

Fargo couldn't argue with that sentiment.

He hustled them on toward the back of the big house. They found a door, or rather an opening where a door had once been. Fargo went first, checking to make sure no one was nearby. Seeing that the way was clear, he waved the young women forward.

"Run for the corral!"

They dashed across the open space, their shadows dark on the ground from the bright morning sunlight.

"Can you ride bareback?" Fargo asked when they reached the corral.

Jessie and Emily both nodded. Fargo grabbed some hackamores that were hanging on the fence and ducked to climb through the rails. He approached a couple of horses that didn't seem too skittish and slipped the hackamores on them. He grasped the ropes attached to the bridles and led the two horses over to the gate.

"Climb up on the fence and get on," Fargo told Jessie and Emily. He held the rifle and the pistol as they did so. When they were mounted, he gave the weapons back to them and said, "I'll open the gate, and you ride hell-for-leather out of here. Head on up the canyon and climb out of it as soon as you get to a good place."

"What about you, Skye?" Jessie asked with a worried frown. "Aren't you coming with us?"

Fargo shook his head. "I'm going to stampede these horses behind you. Then I'm heading back into the house to try to find those cavalry troopers. The Comancheros have them locked up somewhere in there. I plan on us giving the whole bunch enough of a fight that they'll be too busy to come after the two of you."

"Skye, no!" Jessie cried. "You're sacrificing your life for us. You can't do that."

"I can't ride off and leave those soldiers to die, either. Now go on and get out of here while you've got the chance, blast it."

"Skye, I—"

"Ah, hell," Fargo muttered. He swung the gate open and slapped Jessie's horse on the rump, hard, in a continuation of the same motion. The horse leaped into a gallop. Emily followed, but not without a glance of regret toward Fargo.

The other horses might have followed those two anyway, but Fargo made sure of it by running around the edge of the corral and shouting at them. He snatched a couple of rocks from the ground and heaved them at the animals. They poured out through the open gate and began running. Some of them went on up the canyon after Jessie and Emily, while others scattered out and ran toward the front of the hacienda. It wouldn't be long before the Comancheros realized that something was wrong. Fargo dashed toward the house, wanting to get inside so that he could search for those imprisoned soldiers.

Fargo hadn't quite reached the house when he heard a sudden rumbling sound behind him, like distant drums or a lurking thunderstorm. He stopped and turned to gaze up the canyon and felt shock go through him as he saw the huge cloud of dust billowing up. He could think of only one thing that would cause that much dust and that much noise.

A buffalo stampede.

And Jessie and Emily had fled right into the face of it.

They must have seen and heard the stampede coming, Fargo told himself. They would get out of the canyon, out of the way of the onrushing mass of shaggy, maddened death and destruction. If they didn't, they had no chance of escape, and there wasn't a damned thing Fargo could do to help them.

In the meantime, he thought that the old house, even in its

current state of abandonment and disrepair, would stand up to the stampede. The charging buffalo would veer around such a large obstacle in their path. Anyone caught outside, though, would be in serious trouble.

For a moment as he hurried inside, he heard alarmed shouts coming from the Comancheros and their visitors. Then the sound of the stampede rose like a wave and drowned out everything else.

Fargo ducked down a hall he hadn't been in earlier and spotted two men standing in front of a barred door. They held rifles and belonged to the band of Comancheros. When they saw Fargo, they yelled curses and swung their rifles toward him.

Fargo fired the Colt twice before either man could get off a shot. The heavy bullets smashed the men back against the wall behind them. One clutched his chest and fell. The other spun around crazily as blood spewed from his throat where Fargo's slug had torn it open. He collapsed a second later.

Fargo ran along the hall to the door and holstered his gun long enough to grab the thick bar and raise it from its brackets. He stepped back as the door sprang open and the cavalry troopers from Lt. Kemp's patrol scrambled out of their prison. The men stopped short at the sight of Fargo, who nodded toward the two men he had just killed.

"Get their guns," he said. "There are plenty of Comanches and Comancheros outside who are about to come pouring back in."

"What's that sound?" one of the troopers yelled over the rising thunder of the stampede.

"Hell on earth," Fargo said.

He ran toward the front of the house with the troopers straggling along behind him. When Fargo paused as he entered the big main room, he felt the floor vibrating under his feet. The whole world was shaking because of the buffalo—this part of it, anyway.

Several of the Comancheros ran through the front door. The soldiers who had armed themselves stepped up beside Fargo. All of them opened fire, the unexpected shots cutting down the outlaws like a scythe through wheat. Fargo called, "Grab their guns!" and ran toward the men they had just shot down.

He thumbed fresh rounds into the Colt and then bent to pick up a handgun that one of the Comancheros had dropped. With both hands filled, he stepped through the doorway and started thumbing off shots, first from the right hand, then the left, back and forth as muzzle flame spurted from the barrels of the guns. The bullets ripped into the Comanches and Comancheros as they tried to escape the stampede by fleeing into the house. The soldiers began firing from the windows as well, and more of the outlaws and Indians fell.

Some of the Comanches tried to run away from the stampede as it split and flowed around the hacienda like a tidal wave. Not Bitter Wind. Fargo spotted the war chief standing there like he was rooted to the ground in a show of stubborn defiance. Bitter Wind raised his rifle and fired, bringing down the nearest of the charging buffalo. The shaggy beasts behind the fallen one veered around it, and for a second Bitter Wind stood there tall and proud with the buffalo surrounding him.

Then he looked over, saw Fargo, and had just enough time for surprise to register on his face before he went down underneath the thundering hooves that chopped and pounded him into something that wouldn't even look human anymore.

Carl Franklin and Pike Monroe stumbled toward the hacienda. Fargo swung his guns toward them when they were about twenty feet away, but as he pulled the triggers, the hammers of both Colts clicked on empty chambers. Both men grinned as they realized Fargo was out of bullets. Franklin lifted his ivory-handled revolver, while Monroe brought his cavalry carbine to his shoulder.

Instantly, Fargo dropped the empty guns and stooped to jerk the Arkansas toothpick from the sheath on his calf. He didn't have time to draw the knife back and then throw it. He flipped it underhand instead as he straightened, the sort of throw that only a very powerful man could make with such a heavy knife. It flew straight and true, and the blade buried itself in Monroe's chest with a meaty thud. Monroe's eyes widened in shock and pain as he dropped his rifle and staggered to the side. He pawed at the knife's handle but couldn't pull it free. Like a tree in the forest, the burly noncom swayed and then toppled.

But that left Carl Franklin drawing a bead on a now-unarmed Fargo.

A rifle suddenly cracked close by. The heavy slug punched into Franklin's chest and spun him halfway around. He gasped, "You . . . you . . ." The rifle blasted again and hammered him off his feet. He landed in a huddled heap and didn't move again.

Fargo looked over at Jessie Franklin, who stood there holding a rifle as smoke curled from the barrel.

"How the hell—" he began.

Jessie smiled grimly at him as she lowered the weapon. "We turned around and came back before we'd gone very far. We weren't going to just ride off and leave you here to die, Skye. Not after all you've done for us."

The Trailsman grunted. "I reckon we're even. You just saved my life."

By gunning down your own father, he thought.

But it took more than blood to be a father, he reflected, and Carl Franklin had never been anything to Jessie and Emily, any more than he had been to Whit. Not really.

The earthshaking roar of the stampede was dying away now as the buffalo left the canyon and spread out on the flats in front of it. Fargo looked around. He didn't see any Comanches or Comancheros on their feet. He and the troopers had taken care of the ones who hadn't been trampled and flattened by the buffalo. That miracle Jessie had mentioned had sure enough showed up here on a sunny Texas morning.

Or was it purely a miracle? There were buffalo herds in this part of Texas, and the shaggy beasts were prone to stampedes, but what had caused this one at this particular time?

The answer might be on its way. One of the soldiers came running from the rear of the house and said excitedly, "Mr. Fargo, there are a couple of riders comin' in!"

Fargo grinned at Jessie and Emily. "Come on, ladies. I reckon you'll want to see this."

They all went out the back of the hacienda. Jessie and Emily used their hands to shield their eyes as they peered up the canyon at the two men riding closer. The Ovaro walked along, riderless, beside them.

After a moment, Emily exclaimed, "That's Whit!"

"And Lieutenant Kemp," Fargo said. "Looks like you were right about them getting away from those Comancheros."

Whit and Kemp reined in a few moments later and swung down from their saddles to be greeted by hugs from Jessie and Emily and handshakes from Fargo. The troopers gathered around as well, lined up in rough ranks, and then came to attention and saluted Kemp.

The lieutenant returned the salute and said, "At ease, men. It appears that you've done a good job here. Any casualties?"

"A few scratches, Lieutenant," one of the soldiers reported. "And Sergeant Monroe is, well, dead."

Kemp looked shocked. "Dead?"

"Don't let it bother you too much, Lieutenant," Fargo drawled. "Before he crossed the divide, he sold out the patrol to the Comancheros."

Kemp sighed and shook his head. "That's what I was afraid of. I saw him with Franklin and the others through my field glasses, while you were trying to rescue the ladies. I tried to tell myself that he had been taken prisoner, but I think I knew all along that wasn't the case."

Fargo nodded toward the troopers. "I reckon you'd better give one of these fellas a field promotion to corporal or even sergeant, to help you get back to Fort Griffin. They might be inexperienced, but they all handled themselves pretty well from what I saw."

"That's good advice, Mr. Fargo."

"Now, tell me . . . It was you and Whit who started that buffalo stampede, wasn't it?"

A broad grin stretched across Whit's face. "Yeah, we came across that herd grazin' up the canyon after we lit out so those Comancheros wouldn't find us. We hated to leave you like that, Skye, but we figured we might be able to do some good if they didn't capture us, so we dodged 'em and hid out all night. We were heading back this morning when we saw those buffalo."

"It was Whit's idea to stampede them," Kemp said.

"Yeah, but it was the lieutenant who rode right in among 'em to get them started running."

"I'm just glad the two of you showed up when you did, with those shaggy, smelly reinforcements of yours." Fargo went over to the Ovaro and patted the stallion's shoulder. "We'd better go see if we can round up enough mounts to get your men back to the fort. I'm pretty sure all of the horses didn't get caught in the stampede."

"All right," Kemp said as he took up his reins. "But we're not going directly back to Fort Griffin. I thought we'd escort the four of you to this Lost Valley you mentioned, where the Franklin ranch is located. After all, our primary mission is accomplished. The war party that raided down in the Brazos region has been defeated."

"Does this mean I'm not under arrest anymore?" Fargo asked dryly.

Kemp hesitated, then smiled. "I think we can safely say that. You may not have a very high opinion of me, Mr. Fargo, but I assure you, I learn quickly."

"Yeah," Fargo said. "I reckon you do."

Later that morning, after Fargo and Whit had found enough horses for the members of the patrol—some of the original cavalry mounts, and some that had belonged to the Comancheros—the group moved out, leaving the crumbling hacienda and the scene of bloody violence behind them. Fargo and Jessie rode in the lead, followed by Kemp, Whit, Emily, and the rest of the troopers.

"I don't suppose you'd consider staying a while in Lost Valley when we get back," Jessie said quietly.

"We'll have to wait and see," Fargo said . . . but they both knew what his answer really meant.

Jessie, Emily, and Whit would have a lot to hash out

when they got home. They would have to confront their mother with the news that Carl Franklin had been behind the raid on the ranch, as well as his claim that he was really the father of Jessie and Emily. Fargo didn't know how all that would play out, but he was glad he wouldn't have to be part of it. The twisting trails of the human heart were often harder to follow than any frontier path.

And Skye Fargo already felt the longing for the wild country, the free country, where eagles soared through the heavens and the wind carried a siren song that the Trailsman would always answer.

LOOKING FORWARD!
The following is the opening section of the next novel in the exciting *Trailsman* series from Signet:

THE TRAILSMAN #339
RED RIVER RECKONING

Red River Valley, Indian Territory, 1860—
Where a murderous gang of river pirates hold a beautiful woman hostage, and Skye Fargo wages the fight of his life near the famous river that runs red—with blood.

A sudden hell-spawned yell split the silence of the lonely trail, raising the fine hairs on Skye Fargo's arms and tingling his scalp.

"Steady, old campaigner," he soothed his black-and-white pinto stallion as it stutter-stepped nervously backward. "It might kill us, but it won't eat us."

The crop-bearded, buckskin-clad man flicked the riding thong off the hammer of his single-action Colt and filled his hand. He sat his quivering horse in silent patience, shrewd, sun-crinkled, lake blue eyes gazing ahead down a narrow trail.

On his left, a long and steep slope dense with brush and scrub oak led down to a timber-rich stretch of Red River, dividing the Indian Territory from Texas. On his right, the upward slope bristled with thick patches of hawthorn bushes, an ambusher's paradise.

A second time the hideous noise assaulted Fargo's ears—a demonic warbling from just ahead that again spooked the Ovaro. This time, however, Fargo recognized it.

"It's no devil," he assured his horse. "Just sounds like one. That's the Texas yell—but it's on the wrong side of the river."

Fargo hadn't heard the distinctive and unnerving Texas yell in years. The vengeful war cry had arisen after the massacre at the Alamo, and Texas Rangers had put it to good use fighting Kiowas and Comanches. But he never expected to hear it here in The Nations, as most men called the Indian Territory. Now more curious than nervous, Fargo tapped his heels, gigging the Ovaro forward.

Within moments he could hear a man, who sounded drunk as the lords of creation, belting out the lyrics to "Skip to My Lou." The hidden singer, his voice hoarse and rusty, next broke into "What Was Your Name in the States?"

Guiding himself by the awful singing, Fargo soon spotted a wayworn man and horse, both long in the tooth, lying sprawled on the steep slope below. Fargo couldn't see the man's face well under his slouched beaver hat, but his grizzled beard showed more salt than pepper, and a moccasin with a hard sole of buffalo hide covered his exposed right foot.

The horse, a ginger with a white mane, was dead from a broken neck. The man's left leg appeared to be trapped under the animal.

"Hush down, old-timer," Fargo called out. "You couldn't carry a tune in a bucket."

"That's Gospel, stranger, but my screechin' keeps off the buzzards."

"Looks like you could use a hand, old son. You stove up?"

"Nah. That leg's been busted before, and a busted bone knits stronger. But this damn horse has got me pinned."

Fargo leathered his Colt, then swung down and loosened the bridle. He dropped the bit before ground-tethering his stallion.

"I can smell forty-rod from here," he called down. "This ain't no trail to be riding drunk. Bad enough you killed your horse—that could be *your* neck that got snapped."

"No need to fling it in my teeth, boy. I ain't drunk. Would you believe this happened on account I ain't slept in ten whole days?"

"That's flat-out impossible," Fargo said.

"No, it ain't—I sleep at *night*."

The old man grinned broadly at his bad joke while Fargo shook his head. "Skeletons grin just like you are right now, you old fool."

"So what? Way I see it, skeletons ain't nothing but bones with the people scraped off."

"All right, cracker-barrel philosopher, I might's well just leave you where you are."

"Great jumpin' Judas! Don't leave me here, stranger—happens them Staked Plain Comanches find me, they'll slice off my eyelids under this blazin' sun."

"Simmer down, old bird dog. I'm just roweling you. I'll get you out. First I got a signal to send."

From where he stood, on the lip of the sandy trail, Fargo could see a supply-laden keelboat anchored under a white truce flag. He was serving as a contract scout for the freight-hauling firm of Russel, Majors & Waddell, which had recently added keelboats to their line of conveyances. This one was hauling Arkansas goods west to the settlement at Wichita Falls, Texas.

Fargo removed a fragment of mirror from one of his saddle pockets and began flashing it toward the keelboat.

"The hell you doing?" the trapped man demanded.

"See that boat way down there? Whenever I have a line of sight, I signal the all-secure to them."

"All secure, my sweet aunt."

"Spell that out," Fargo said, still flashing.

"Well, there's some stink brewing up in these parts, but I ain't caught a clear whiff of it yet."

"There's *always* stink brewing up in The Nations," Fargo reminded him. "That's been true ever since the government set it aside for the tribes. The place is an owlhoot paradise. By law, no Indian council can prosecute whites, and white man's law won't serve warrants on white criminals holed up here. Which leads a man to wonder what *you're* doing here."

"You an Indian lover? You didn't mention nothin' about red criminals."

"Quit dodging. What are you doing here?"

"Right now I'm laid out under a dead horse. You gonna help me or just stand there poking into my backtrail?"

Fargo waited for a return signal from the boat. The vessel was fifty-five feet long, with shallow sides that sloped inward. These formed a pen for the horses and mules grouped tightly behind a plank cabin amidships.

Fargo got the signal and put the mirror away. "No need to get all lathered up. Here I come."

Bracing his leg muscles against the steep angle, using sturdy brush for handholds, Fargo scrambled down. As he drew nearer, he saw the old roadster was an unequivocally homely man with coarse-grained skin, a careworn face, and a hawk nose.

"You ever hear of soap?" Fargo complained as he reached the trapped man's location. This close, he could see beggar-lice leaping from his clothing. "There's a stink around here, all right."

"I *am* a mite ripe," the man admitted. "I got no supplies. What's your name, son?"

Fargo knelt to get a closer look at the trapped leg. "Fargo. Skye Fargo."

The old man started. "Fargo? The same hombre some calls the Trailsman?"

"'Fraid so. I think I can lift this carcass up just enough for you to pull out from under it. It's only trapping your foot."

"Skye Fargo?" the old man wondered aloud. "So *you're* the one can read sign on bare rock and track an ant across desert hardpan, huh?"

"Sure, and I can turn burro piss into wine, too. Never mind all that. . . . When I heave, jerk your foot out."

Fargo put his back to the horse's withers, took hold, and heaved, taut muscles straining like steel cables.

"Got 'er!" the old salt cried out jubilantly. He sat up, massaging his left foot. "You're strong as horseradish, Fargo."

"What's your name?" Fargo asked.

"Rip Miller. Ripley Alexander Miller the Third, to chew it fine."

Fargo snorted. "That's a thirty-five-cent mouthful. Rip is fine with me. Well, Rip, a word to the not-so-wise: You're out of your latitude here, pop."

"Pop? Boy, a man is only as old as the women he feels."

Fargo fought back a grin, telling himself to remember that one. "Like I said, you're out of your latitude. Drunken saddle tramps don't stand a snowball's chance in The Nations."

"Saddle tramp? Hell's fire, you mouthy pup! Boy, I was scalpin' Kiowas while you was still on ma's milk. Why, Rip Miller would wink into a rifle barrel. Saddle tramp, my sweet aunt. I prefer to call myself a bachelor of the saddle—same as you, from what I hear."

"If you're such a rip-snortin' *bravo*, the hell you doing slinking around the Indian Territory?"

"On account I got drunk and burnt down a boardinghouse in Missouri, that's why. Strictly an accident, y'unnerstan'. Left Sedalia just ahead of a warrant."

"Like I figured—another damned owlhoot." In spite of himself, Fargo felt sorry for the old coot. He helped him to his feet. "How's that foot feel?"

"A mite ginger, but she'll come sassy. My cave ain't but a whoop and a holler from here, happens you don't mind riding double."

"You'll want this saddle," Fargo said.

"For a fact. Last thing I own. It's my rocking chair by day, my pillow by night."

Fargo undid the cinch and jerked the saddle free. He noticed the high, narrow horn and the *cabristra* coiled around it, a hair rope of the Texas style.

"Sorry about your horse," Fargo said, lugging the saddle over one shoulder and helping Rip up the slope with his free arm.

"Ah, that spavined son of a bitch never missed a chance to bite me on the ass. Won him in a poker game, and I'm glad to be shut of him."

They were just reaching the lip of the trail when Fargo's Ovaro gave his trouble whicker, a sound the Trailsman had learned over the years to respect. The two men gained the trail, and Fargo spotted them immediately: buzzards wheeling in the soft blue sky to the west, dark harbingers of death.

"Pile on the agony," he muttered.

"Could be a dead buff," Rip suggested. "Plenty around here."

"Could be," Fargo agreed, helping the old man up first.

But as Fargo turned the stirrup around and stepped into it, then pushed up and over, he couldn't help admitting it to himself: Trouble liked to dog the Trailsman like an afternoon shadow, and whatever waited for him up ahead, it was surely no dead buffalo.

"That stink you claimed is brewing up," Fargo said after they'd ridden for a few minutes. "You talking about Indian trouble or white-man trouble?"

"Both, likely. Been a lot more gunfire lately. All the tribes here in The Nations signed the Laramie Treaty back in 'fifty-one, but some just done it to get the presents. They never accepted the terms."

Fargo nodded. He'd fought renegades here before. "You saying some tribes have struck the war trail?"

"Nah, but some of the heap-big chiefs like Yellow Bear of the Staked Plain Comanches took their clans and jumped the rez. Now they like to swoop in here from the Texas Panhandle. They hit fast and hightail it back to the Llano."

Fargo's slitted gaze stayed in constant motion. Red River was out of sight on their left now as the trail passed through sandy, hilly terrain interspersed with pines and granite cliffs. He could still see the buzzards, circling lower and lower.

"Folks cry you up big, Fargo," Rip said.

"Yeah, in the same newspapers they use to wipe their asses."

The smelly old drifter chuckled. "Both of us—dead broke and famous. Ain't it pitiful?"

"What makes you famous—the stench blowing off you?"

"If youth but knew. Sonny boy, you ever heard of Bob Coleman?"

"Who hasn't?" Fargo replied. "He was the first captain of the Texas Rangers."

"Ahuh, and I rode with him from 'thirty-five to 'thirty-nine. Fought Lipan Apaches, Kiowas, Comanches, and Mexers. Back then we didn't have Sam Colt's fancy revolvers like the one you got strapped on. Us Rangers was the best fighters and the best troublemakers."

"Best riders, too?" Fargo jibed. "Hell, Rip, that trail you fell off was twelve feet wide. Any fool could see the lip was loose sand."

"Pipe down, you jay! A jackrabbit spooked my horse."

"It's past mending now," Fargo relented. "I don't like all this screening timber. Stow the chinwag and keep that dragoon pistol of yours to hand."

They were riding nearer to whatever trouble lay ahead,

and Fargo palmed the cylinder of his Colt to check the loads. Then he loosened his 16-shot, brass-framed Henry rifle in its saddle boot.

When the Ovaro began to sidestep, reluctant to proceed, Fargo felt a stirring of belly flies. His stallion was one to keep up the strut, and when he shied like this, Fargo knew trouble was on the spit.

"Steady, old warhorse," he soothed, patting the Ovaro's neck.

The rutted trail took a dogleg turn around a copse of pine trees. The sight that greeted both men, when they cleared the turn, made Fargo's gorge rise.

"God's trousers," Rip said in a voice just above a whisper. "Whoever done this ain't even fit to be called pond scum."

Fargo counted three dead men, one still slumped on the seat of a heavy freight wagon. All three sported numerous bullet wounds, some astoundingly large, and had taken finishing shots in the forehead at close range—Fargo could see the powder burns on their skin.

"Shot to rag tatters," Rip said, anger tightening his voice. "Whoever done it even killed the horses."

Both men remained mounted, taking a careful look around.

"Like I was sayin'," Rip spoke up, "Comanches like to swoop into Red River country from the Llano. Goddamn featherheads. Neither Gospel nor gunpowder will ever tame them red devils."

"Red men didn't do this," Fargo gainsaid. "They'd use arrows and war hatchets for a job this easy. Besides, they never waste bullets on horses."

"I take your point. 'Sides, Comanches woulda lifted their dander and cut off their pizzles. These poor devils ain't been touched 'cept by bullets."

Fargo lit down and gave Rip a hand dismounting. Then the Trailsman began walking slow circles around the area, reading the signs.

"Four riders on shod horses," he concluded. "And at least

one more driving a wagon. The wagon ruts are shallow coming in from the west, deeper heading back. They cleaned out whatever cargo was in this wagon."

"No damn wonder these boys couldn't defend theirselves," Rip said, picking up an old German fowling piece. "This old relic ain't much better'n a peashooter."

Fargo knelt to examine one of the corpses. "It didn't happen all that long ago. The blood's just now turning tacky."

Hearing this, Rip glanced nervously all around them. "Happens that's so, then ain't we paring the cheese might close to the rind? Fargo, I fair got the fidgets. Them killers coulda left a rear guard, and he could be droppin' a bead on *us* right now. Let's rustle."

Fargo nodded, standing back up. "They might've played it that way to make sure they get away with the freight—say, what's that?"

A sheet of paper protruding from a dead man's pocket had caught Fargo's eye. He pulled it out and unfolded it. It was an official right-of-transit letter bearing the Bureau of Indian Affairs seal.

"That's what I figured," he told Rip. "These were civilian contract freighters. Every spring they bring in the issue of annuities to the rez Indians. Blankets, coffee, flour, sugar, bacon, and such. We best—"

A bullet tore through the letter in Fargo's hand and thwacked into the freight wagon less than a heartbeat before the crack of a high-power rifle reached both men. The slug was so big it tore out a fist-sized chunk of the wood.

"Hell's a-poppin'!" Rip shouted, scrambling under the wagon as another bullet snapped past Fargo's head, so close he felt a line of heat.

"A writer in the tradition of Louis L'Amour and Zane Grey!"
—*Huntsville Times*

National Bestselling Author
RALPH COMPTON

AUTUMN OF THE GUN
THE KILLING SEASON
THE DAWN OF FURY
BULLET CREEK
RIO LARGO
DEADWOOD GULCH
A WOLF IN THE FOLD
TRAIL TO COTTONWOOD FALLS
BLUFF CITY
THE BLOODY TRAIL
SHADOW OF THE GUN
DEATH OF A BAD MAN
RIDE THE HARD TRAIL
BLOOD ON THE GALLOWS
BULLET FOR A BAD MAN
THE CONVICT TRAIL
RAWHIDE FLAT
OUTLAW'S RECKONING
THE BORDER EMPIRE
THE MAN FROM NOWHERE
SIXGUNS AND DOUBLE EAGLES
BOUNTY HUNTER

GRITTY WESTERN ACTION FROM

USA TODAY BESTSELLING AUTHOR

RALPH COTTON

FAST GUNS OUT OF TEXAS

KILLING TEXAS BOB

NIGHTFALL AT LITTLE ACES

AMBUSH AT SHADOW VALLEY

RIDE TO HELL'S GATE

GUNMEN OF THE DESERT SANDS

SHOWDOWN AT HOLE-IN-THE-WALL

RIDERS FROM LONG PINES

CROSSING FIRE RIVER

ESCAPE FROM FIRE RIVER

Available wherever books are sold or at penguin.com